A Divine Christmas Ghost Story

BOOK III

Printed in the United States of America.

ISBN: 978-1-63385-507-6

Library of Congress Control Number: 2023922658

Illustration by: Teresa Emeloff

Layout and Design by Jason Price

Published by:

Word Association Publishers

205 Fifth Avenue

Tarentum, Pennsylvania 15084

www.wordassociation.com

1.800.827.7903

A Divine Christmas Ghost Story

BOOK III

Robert Cameron Malcolm IV

Illustrations by: Teresa Emeloff

Acknowledgements and Dedication

As in my previous books, a special thanksgiving goes out to Mr. Jeffrey Andrew Yeager, Laurie Malcolm, and Teresa Emeloff for their help with this novella. Jeff, my college roommate and friend, not only provided critical review of this story, but also performed the task of editing. His comments, suggestions, and keen insights are always welcome and most helpful. Teresa Emeloff, whose marvelous illustrations are featured on the first page of each chapter, has been a great help to me in spreading the word about this novella. I deeply appreciate her enthusiasm and delight in helping me with this book. Laurie, my wife, also provided critical review of this novella as well as aided in its editing.

Thanksgiving also is extended to the fine people of Costello Printing and Word Association Publishers in Tarentum, Pennsylvania, for all their suggestions and help. Their enthusiasm and encouragement are infectious!

I am also thankful for the help of the Reverend Jeffrey Scott Wylie, Rector of Christ's Church (ACNA) in Greensburg, Pennsylvania. His help and encouragement aided my efforts in developing this story.

It must be noted that the *Church of the Transfiguration* is purely fictional, as well as the other Anglican churches mentioned in this book. The ACNA was chosen as the denominational setting for all three books that have been written thus far, due to the author's respect for their Church.

There are also several other individuals, who are unnamed here, whose contribution to this book have been helpful. Together, we shared a significant part of the story which is represented in this book. While parts of this tale are mythological, there is also a great deal of historical truth behind parts of the story. This book is dedicated to those unnamed individuals who labored with me "side by side" during my career in the battle against the dark forces aligned against our Christ. One individual, in particular, comes to mind as we struggled together to forever free her from the entities that afflicted her. All of us look forward to that day and time when the cosmic war, as depicted in the Bible, is over and our God and His Christ reign unhindered and supreme. We also look forward to that new era when human beings aligned with Christ are no longer subjected to the malady of the dark forces arrayed against us.

Contents

Preface

This novella represents the third installment in the *Divine Christmas Ghost Story Series. A Divine Christmas Ghost Story: Book Three,* is the conclusion of the spiritual warfare between a divine representative and a representative of the cosmic rebellion. The concept of spiritual warfare is uncomfortable to most Christians. Few adherents of the faith know much about it, and those who do prefer to avoid the subject. While some of the material presented in this book represents actual events, not everything known to the author about the subject matter is included here. This is one of many areas of ministry that the author surrendered upon retirement.

Once again, besides the entertainment value of this story, a greater purpose of this novella, like the two before it, is to provoke some thought and commentary on church and culture during this time in American history. It is the hope of the author that some of the biblical teaching, church practice, church tradition, and speculation about life after this life highlighted here will be beneficial to the reader.

Enjoy the book, and as Charles Dickens stated about his *Christmas Carol,* "…May it haunt their houses pleasantly and no one wish to lay it!"

Stave 1
Flushed

lushed from the former boat ramp at Tarentum Riverview Park, the extraordinarily malicious demonic entity known as "The Lady of the Church" was thrust down the Allegheny River by a thunderous, tumbling, and tumultuous flow of water. This rolling current, which gushed high into the air and sprayed white foam as it travelled downstream, only impacted the river in the immediate vicinity of the witch-like manifestation as it was being expelled from the towns of Tarentum and Creighton. The evil spirit found no respite as it passed Arnold and New Kensington. It finally came to rest nearly 9 miles downstream on the upper half of the split Fourteen Mile Island, just above the 1932 Allegheny River Lock and Dam #3 which is now named for C. W. "Bill" Young. Being thrown forcefully onto the island and crash landing amid much brush and tree branches, the malevolent spirit transformed itself out of its physical appearance taking on invisibility once more. Ascending into the air, the demonic entity took stock of its surroundings. On the western shore of the river lay Harmar Township, with Cheswick and Springdale adjacent to it. On the eastern shore lay Plum Borough with the heights of Coxcomb Hill towering above the river. It was there that the unclean spirit saw an impressive edifice with two illuminated steeples shining in the darkness.

The Church of the Transfiguration was an impressive Anglican Church. It stood way above the river on a very high and steep hill. The view from the church was remarkable, especially looking westward during sunset. The church was rightly named, for it appeared to the people in the towns below to be high upon a mountaintop. When its original and longtime congregation could no longer afford its upkeep due to slumping membership and attendance, the Anglican Church of North America purchased it and sought to renew the site affiliated with their recent denominational establishment. The first rector of the newly organized congregation was a married priest known as Alexander Andrew McKenzie. A conservative biblically and theologically, he had left a liberal Presbyterian denomination and was received by the ACNA. Alex was married to the former Annalena Layne Whitworth. The couple had two infant twin sons: Theodore and Truman. They also had a daughter named Kendall who was two years old. They resided in the rectory located near the church, and enjoyed its location except in the wintertime when the steep roads going up and down Coxcomb Hill made travel difficult during inclement weather.

Alex, as he was commonly called, was 6 foot, 2 inches tall. He had brown hair and brown eyes and was of medium build. He had worn spectacles since the fourth grade. While he was not an athlete, he was strong, fit, and capable of accomplishing much physical labor. He enjoyed hiking in the wilderness, mountaineering, and technical rock climbing. His heritage was primarily Scottish. He was an articulate and expressive man who was accomplished in the pulpit. Excelling in both speaking and writing, he could be serious and then instantaneously flip into the humorous. He was popular with both the adults and the children of his congregation. He was non-condescending with the children and teenagers under his charge, and enjoyed sharing self-deprecating humor with them. Alex had graduated from Westminster College in New Wilmington, PA and secured a Master of Divinity degree attending seminary in Pittsburgh.

His wife of several years, Annalena, had grown up in Western Pennsylvania. Like her husband, she too had brown hair and brown eyes. She had studied business in college, but flipped to clementary education half way through her under-graduate experience. Annalena enrolled at Grove City College, but transferred to Westminster when she changed majors. She met Alex at a dance they both attended while she was at Grove City. They started dating and rapidly grew to love each other. It is a fact that their budding romance did have something to do with Annalena's transfer to be on the same campus as her beloved. The two made a handsome couple. Annalena was quite good looking with splendid feminine features. While she grew up as a Christian, Alex had a great deal of influence on her spiritual development and growing interest in studying the Bible. The couple became engaged while at Westminster and planned to marry only when Alex finished seminary. Waiting proved to be too difficult for them to endure, due to their intense affection for each other, and so before Alex finished his education they tied the marital knot. They had a beautiful Celtic style wedding and were most delighted with each other. During those years, Annalena took a teaching position with the Fox Chapel School District at Kerr Elementary School. She became an excellent instructor teaching second grade and was very popular with her students, their parents, her colleagues, and the administration. In the new fledgling church, she served in many capacities but was careful not to involve herself in any decision making and drama which often, unfortunately, accompanies church membership. With two twin toddlers and a daughter to raise, she was too busy to get involved in those things which "major in the minors".

While the congregation was too small and financially challenged to afford an assistant minister, the Vestry permitted a young man named Ian Kellen McKallip to serve and receive training at the church as a seminarian. Ian brought with him his girlfriend, Brienne Noelle Way to the church. It did not take long for Annalena and Brienne to get acquainted and become good friends. Brienne was a towering young woman. She was every inch of six feet tall. She was an attractive young lady who possessed a pleasing personality. She was always smiling and her face seemed to beam both joy and mirth. She was friendly, and in spite of some shyness, she became well regarded in the church. Ian was not a tall man. In fact, he was four inches shorter than his girlfriend. He was generally regarded by others as being a handsome young man. He also did not seem to mind that he sported red hair, though he was teased about his appearance throughout his childhood. Regardless of their height difference, the two of them made a most pleasing presentation of themselves.

When Alex became the rector of the Church of the Transfiguration, one of his childhood friends decided to follow him to this parish. Her name was Katrina Brynlee McLaren Helman. The two of them met in kindergarten and were classmates throughout their grammar school and high school years. Katrina was a short woman with jet black eyes and long black hair. After high school, she entered into the medical profession and studied nursing. She eventually became a physician's assistant. She was well educated and very sharp mentally. During her education she met her future husband, Hugh Hector Helman. Hugh was an affable fellow who also worked in the medical field. Like Ian, he too was short, but also like Ian he was perceived by those who got to know him to be a rather handsome man. Eventually the two of them gave birth to a daughter. They named their daughter, Moriah.

Alex and Katrina attended the same youth group in a Presbyterian Church in Natrona Heights throughout their middle school and high school years. During these seven years, they learned much about Jesus Christ, the Bible, ethics, mission, and the Christian way of life. In fact, during high school, they participated in a couple of mission trips with their youth group. One such trip was to Trenton, New Jersey where they volunteered for a week at the East Trenton Habitat for Humanity Center doing construction. During this trip, they stayed at a host church which helped to sponsor their mission effort. Both Alex and Katrina came to believe that the church they stayed in was haunted. Not only did they have a feeling in certain areas of the church of being watched, but the cemetery which rested on two sides of the church appeared to be – well, let's just say – supernaturally active during the night. The church really "spooked them out," as people are wont to say, as the two of them experienced one moment of real terror in the night which they attempted to forget and put behind them. It was an experience that they never talked about. It was an occurrence that neither of them could dismiss from their memory. It was a circumstance that they soon would be forced to deal with in a profound way.

Hugh and Katrina united with the church and immediately became very involved. Katrina began working with the newly created youth groups and with other fellowship organizations within the church. She became very popular as she was very effective in helping people and giving them wise counsel. Hugh became involved in helping with the building and the property, but lent his assistance as well to those things in which Katrina was active. Katrina's ministry, even though she could be soft-spoken and somewhat reserved, produced a great harvest for the Christ. She had a real passion for the things of God, and intelligently so! The results of her dedication and efforts for Jesus were certain to capture the attention of Christ's opposition.

On that fateful day in Advent, wherein the familiar spirit had been cast down river from Tarentum in a very violent way by Jillian Julianna Jiganie and the unseen forces of heaven, the Lady of the Church knew that she was unable to travel upstream to once more engage in her chaotic and destructive behavior. The words pronounced at the time of her expulsion from Tarentum Riverview Park forbade her from returning. These words spiritually locked her out and away from any kind of operation in that area. Once pronounced, the declaration was backed up and secured by heavenly forces which were far too powerful for her to overcome. There was nothing, however, that prevented her from creating mischief in this area northeast of Pittsburgh. As she flew around The Church of the Transfiguration, she discovered it to be an Anglican church. This church would probably make a good target for her evil machinations. The demon's task was to attempt to neutralize and destroy anything that elevated God and His Christ. Doing so in particularly conservative Christian churches, which were the most dangerous to her Lord and Prince, were very enticing. Entering the Church of the Transfiguration, the demon decided to assess the congregation, its leadership, and its membership to see if there was any opening which she could exploit to allow her to practice her macabre and wretched arts. The Lady of the Church would find this church and its people very conducive for the mayhem she enjoyed conjuring.

The outcome of the event of one spiritual battle would now lead, unintentionally, to another great conflict with an additional church downriver. So, it was here on the heights above the Allegheny River, wherein the lives of the McKenzies, the Helmans, Ian McKallip, Brienne Way, among others, would discover a significant challenge to their peace, persons, and relationships which they had to overcome and remove from their presence.

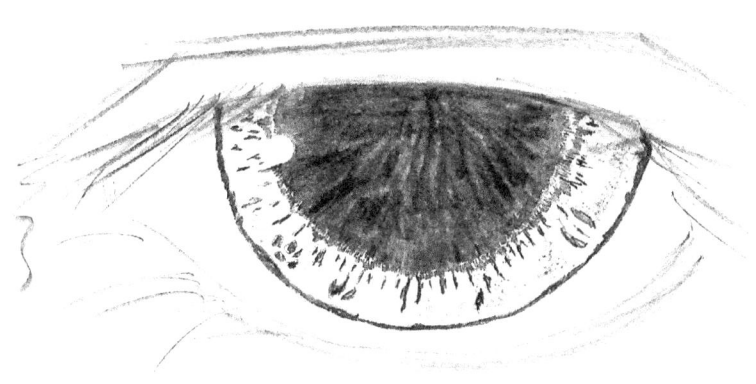

Stave 2

Whitewing Luster
and the Green Eye

he *Lady of the Church* settled into her new surroundings. She discovered that the Church of the
Transfiguration contained a number of people who previously had some experience with the occult. Once an individual
opens that door, they never know what they might find on the
other side. Experiences such as playing with the Ouija Board,

participating in seances, listening to questionable music, and seeking out a psychic can open one up to demonic exposure, activity, and oppression. Like many churches in this period of time, many of the worshippers came to Transfiguration carrying a great deal of baggage from poor decision making in life. Their hollow souls were searching for fulfillment and satisfaction. Unable to find it in the things of this world, the search turned back to God to fill up the vacuum they felt in their empty lives. Each of us has a God-hole in our beings that only a relationship with God can fill. True wisdom is making that discovery and allowing God to occupy the void located in the core of our being.

It was in this setting and circumstance that the *Lady of the Church* first made her presence known. Katrina had arrived at Transfiguration early on a Friday afternoon to begin preparations for a middle school youth group lock-in or sleepover. As Katrina entered the building, she encountered a man known as Jimmy Mack and his business assistant and second-in-command, Audrey Marie Simpson. Katrina had never seen them before and inquired as to their presence in the church at this time. They were very involved in what appeared to be an examination of the building. They were looking up and down, over and around everything. Jimmy Mack was doing most of the talking and Audrey was jotting things down on her device.

"Hello," exclaimed Katrina. "Is there anything I can help you with?" she asked.

"Hi, my name is Jimmy Mack and this is my partner Audrey. We own and operate 'Whitewing Luster', a cleanin' service out of Saxonburg. Fodder McKenzie has us lookin' over dis here church thinkin' he might hire our professional cleanin' services."

At this point, Audrey handed Katrina a business card which included a curious sentence which read, "Whitewing Luster, experts in Purgation, Lustration, Ablution, Lavation, Sanitation, Disinfection, Fumigation, and Irrigation." Katrina thought their card to be quite curious. She would need to consult a dictionary to understand it. "Maybe that was the point of it all," she thought to herself.

"Wherever did you come up with the name 'Whitewing Luster'?" asked Katrina.

Audrey responded, "The name 'whitewing' comes from an individual in yesteryear who was a street sweeper wearing a white uniform. We thought the name was a good fit for a professional cleaning service. We take great pride in our work. Our employees will get this church clean and keep it clean, I guarantee you!"

"My, you two are certainly very confident, that's good to know," stated Katrina. "This church has not been too successful at finding or retaining a custodian; hopefully, you can do better!"

"We will," pronounced Audrey confidently.

Just then a cackle, followed by a shriek, echoed through the building. The trio looked up in the direction of the noise to spy a dark, shadowy, translucent figure moving through the trusses of the nave above them.

Jimmy Mack cried out, "Whoa dude, not again! I seen this here black thing before at Holy Trinity Church in Saxonburg several years ago. Look out," shouted Jimmy, "it looks like it's goin' to swoosh down upon us!"

Immediately the figure flew down toward them.

"Duck!" cried out Jimmy Mack as both Audrey and Katrina screamed in unison. The figure, in an instant, proceeded to encircle them, flying faster and faster around them.

Then all of a sudden it went high into the air, turned, and dove straight for Katrina traveling through her and immediately disappeared.

"Where'd it go?" asked Jimmy Mack in a shout. "Did ya see what I seen? Just like in Saxonburg it was like a black veil blowin' arahnd an' arahnd."

Hearing the screams, Father Alex came running from his study into the sanctuary. "What's going on here! What's the matter? I heard screaming! Is everything alright?" he asked the trio as both Audrey and Katrina were holding each other shaking violently.

Jimmy Mack responded, "This here figure swooshed down on us and flew arahnd and arahnd us. Then it dove into Katrina here and we seen it no more."

Father Alex approached Katrina asking, "Are you Ok?"

Katrina immediately left the embrace of Audrey and clung fast to Alex and responded saying, "I don't know, this was the scariest thing I have ever seen since – since, well, you know."

"Yes, I do," replied Alex with his arms wrapped around Katrina.

"Fodder Alex," interjected Jimmy Mack, "this place is givin' me the creeps. Our deal is no deal until ya gits rid of this here ting. We had this here ting happen at Holy Trinity. Ya better call Fodder Dave there and see how they rids 'emselves of it. It might even be the same ting. Yes, call Fodder Dave. When ya gits rid of it, call me. We ain't workin' here until ya do!"

With that Jimmy Mack and Audrey made a direct beeline for the exit, leaving the building in a very hurried fashion.

Alex then pushed Katrina from him. Holding her shoulders in his hands, he bent down and looked directly into her face saying, "Are you ok? Do you want to talk about this? I certainly want you to tell me everything you heard and saw. Here, let's go to my office. You can have a seat and let's get you calmed down."

"I don't think I'm going to calm down anytime soon, Alex. This is all too frightening and what happened at the end really scared me," responded Katrina. "This was just like the experience on that mission trip in the cemetery."

Moving to Alex's office, Katrina proceeded to share the entire moment of horror with him. Needing to talk further, she recounted the haunting experiences they shared on that mission trip earlier in their lives.

"I never truly got over the experiences you and I shared in New Jersey," remarked Katrina. "They haunt me to this day. Do you ever have nightmares about it?"

"I certainly do, at least from time to time," replied Alex. "I have a very vivid dream life. Often it seems so real. It's like that Sean Connery, James Bond movie entitled *You Only Live Twice*. If I remember the title song correctly, I think the idea was that a person's second life was their dream life. In certain respects, that might be true of me. I guess it might be true as you as well. Is it?"

"Yes, it is," stated Katrina forthrightly. "I remember the church we stayed in so well. It had that one hallway which connected the old building with the new educational and fellowship wing. Every time you and I were in it we thought we were being watched. It gave me chills. The hallway was cold and you just got the feeling that something untoward was present with you. We were not the only ones who felt that way. The entire group, including the adults, felt a strange presence in that connecting hallway as well. No one wanted to pass through it alone."

"You got that right," piped in Alex.

"And then, do you remember their youth group room deep in the bowels of that old church building well below the sanctuary? That youth group room gave me the jitters as well. Do you remember the green eye that was painted several places in the room?" asked Katrina.

"Yeah, I do. It was a bit unnerving," responded Alex.

"Unnerving is not quite the word for it, it was terrifying," said Katrina with a shudder in her voice. "Our adult chaperones thought it represented the 'all seeing eye' like on the dollar bill. Some of them thought it was a 'God's Eye' that crafters make. The 'all seeing eye', appears in many cultures throughout antiquity and has connections with witchcraft, the occult, and Masonry. What we did not know at the beginning of the week was that the youth group members of that church who painted it, were doing so because of the experiences they were having in the cemetery adjacent to the building."

"Yeah, what was really spooky," offered Alex as he continued, "was the fact that graves and tombstones were right up against the southern wall of the church building. That was macabre and unsettling to me. On the other side of the wall was that great caged pit of the furnace room wherein they kept their boiler. Do you remember how deep in the ground that went? The fact that they had it all caged in with strong fencing-wire was just plain weird. I guess it was to keep people from falling."

"Of course, I do," replied Katrina. "There was a very skinny passageway around it. I think the original church burned down in a fire. Maybe the people who built it this way just overcompensated when they rebuilt the church on the same spot."

"It certainly reminded me of a vision of hell," stated Alex. "It was dark, lonely, and foreboding. I would hate to see it in operation during the winter. I would imagine that the entire cavern probably is ablaze, reflecting the fire in the furnace. The furnace was also huge and imposing. If that thing ever blew up, 'stop, drop, and roll' would do you no good."

"You are right, and come to think of it, 'stop, drop, and roll' would do one no good in hell. We've got to remember to use that idea with our youth groups," remarked Katrina.

"As spooky as the church buildings were inside, it was the outside that really has haunted us right into our adult lives," stated Alex as he leaned back in his office chair. "During our stay, we played games in the cemetery at night. We even had a kid – remember Robert?" queried Alex. "He tried to scare all of us. Remember when Dennis and Kevin decided to sleep in the cemetery one night? Do you remember how they came rushing in to tell us that they were not alone out there? They were scared out of their wits. It took the adults a while to calm them down. Even then, they had trouble sleeping. But no, you and I had to go out by ourselves to investigate."

"And what did we see?" asked Katrina noticeably uncomfortable with the thought. "Deep inside the cemetery along its main gravel lane we spied a green object hanging in the air. The object was small, but it faced us and began coming our way, picking up speed as it went. Remember, we just stood there mesmerized, watching it coming toward us. Then we wanted to run, but our legs wouldn't move. We just kept staring at it until it was almost upon us. We ducked as it passed over us and then it swept around and around us. I screamed and latched onto you causing the two of us to fall to the ground. I rolled over onto my back. The green thing kept swirling around us until it stopped and hovered over us for several seconds. It was in the shape of an eye. It just stared at us. All of a sudden it dropped down on us and then disappeared. I screamed again, and this time some of the adults and our peers ran out of the church and found us lying on the ground."

"Yeah, they thought we were up to no good. One female adult leader - I will not mention her name, but you know who – thought I was sexually assaulting you. She always came to quick conclusions about things, and most of the time she was wrong," offered Alex.

"True," affirmed Katrina. "They separated us, and then they had each of us tell them our story by ourselves. I don't know if they believed us or not, but at least they concluded that we were not doing anything immoral."

"We were worse than Dennis and Kevin for the rest of that night," remarked Alex. "We did not venture into that cemetery for the remainder of the week."

"But Alex," remarked Katrina in a very serious tone, "what happened to the green eye? It dropped upon us and disappeared. Did it simply vanish? Did it fly through us? Or did it enter us and leave something behind? "

"I don't think it came home with us," replied Alex. "If it had, we would have noticed something all these years, but perhaps you are right – maybe it – well – left something with us or gathered some information about us. I can't say. I just don't know!"

"What bothers me, Alex, is that what happened in the sanctuary a little bit ago reminded me of the green eye. Whatever that shadowy figure was, it flew into me and we never saw it again. There was no indication that it flew out of me. I'm worried, Alex," a quivering Katrina stated frankly to her friend.

"I'm here for you Katrina," said Alex. "Let's pray about this before we start setting up for the sleepover. I've got to think on this for a while. Maybe Jimmy Mack is right. Maybe I need to call Father Dave at Holy Trinity. Remind me why we decided to schedule a youth group sleepover so close to Christmas. This is a busy season for everyone. I'll get in touch with David in the week after Christmas Day. Hopefully, nothing else will happen until then. Let's make sure, however, that we keep a good eye on things tonight and also make certain that none of the youth are alone without adult leadership in the sanctuary. Boy, do I wish that this church had a gymnasium."

"You know, I wish this church had a shower room. We get pretty dirty doing projects here. A shower room would be good when housing other groups for a night or several days," offered Katrina.

"Just a shower room?" laughed Alex. "I wish this church had a hot tub. Wouldn't that be enjoyable if the staff could relax in a hot tub following a youth group event?"

"I know how you could get one," offered Katrina.

"How?" asked Alex.

"I know we are not Baptists, but just say that it could be used for believer baptisms by immersion," giggled Katrina.

"That's a great idea," replied Alex with an expression of deep thought on his face. "I'm going to have to think on that one!"

With that moment of mirth, the two of them went off to make preparations for the sleepover.

Stave 3

ᴛꜰe Sleepover

The sleepover that Alex, Katrina, Ian, Brienne, and the rest of the adult youth group leadership sponsored started off well. A time of all group gaming had been planned. A board game competition was held, as well as a "Wacky Olympics" which commanded and dominated a lot of time. The youth group staff kept the middle schoolers very active. As the hour approached midnight, there was karaoke in the sanctuary using the new and up-to-date production and sound system. Everyone was enjoying the event and having a great deal of fun. The plan for the evening was to quiet things down after one or two AM. In order to do so, a movie was played on a monitor in the undercroft as the youth began to slowly settle down and fall asleep on the floor in their sleeping bags.

During all the singing and chuckling and joy and mirth, while the adults and the youth shared in karaoke, Katrina and Brienne sat in the middle of the sanctuary very engaged in conversation with each other. They laughed as they watched the singing and dancing antics of the youth, Alex, and Ian. Slowly Brienne began to notice that Katrina had become quiet. The joy that Katrina was sharing in conversation and laughter disappeared. Brienne noticed that Katrina sat there almost with a lifeless expression on her face. No longer was she moving. It seemed like she was staring out into space and at nothing in particular.

"Katrina, are you alright?" asked Brienne.

Brienne received no response from Katrina.

"You must be very tired by now, I suppose," continued Brienne. "Well, it will soon be time to quiet them down. You can get some rest. I'll stay up with some of the staff to make sure everything is fine and appropriate with the youth."

Once more, Brienne received no response.

"Katrina – Katrina," called out Brienne turning her body in the pew and rotating her face closer to her co-volunteer. "Is something wrong? Why are you not answering me?"

Just then Katrina turned her face toward Brienne. Katrina's face was expressionless. Her eyes seemed soulless and vacant. Then, without saying a word, she jerked her head in a strange maneuver and continued staring straight ahead.

"Did I say something that offended you, Katrina?" asked Brienne. "Why have you become so quiet?"

At that, Katrina once again, oddly with a clear jerking motion, turned her head toward Brienne. This time she blinked several times and seemed to come out of a world of unknowing and back into reality again.

"Did you say something to me, Brienne?" asked Katrina.

"Yes, I did several times. Are you feeling fine?" inquired Brienne.

"Yes, I am feeling well. Why do you ask?" responded Katrina.

"You were acting strange there for a little bit. I was concerned that something might be wrong with you," stated Brienne.

"No, I am all right," countered Katrina. "What time is it anyway? It is probably time to wrap this up and get the kids moving downstairs. Excuse me, but I am going to see if Alex is ready to end karaoke and take them to the fellowship hall."

With that, Katrina moved past Brienne in the pew. As she walked down the aisle to the chancel area, Brienne noticed a couple of odd jerks Katrina made in her movement. Brienne curiously cocked her head to her left side and then shrugged her shoulders.

Brienne hoped that the rest of the night would be uneventful. She noticed, however, strange occurrences surrounding Katrina in the dimly lit undercroft as the youth group members nestled down to sleep. Alex was on the other side of the room. He was the primary leader in charge and had to stay awake all night. Katrina was asleep on the floor not far from Brienne. Ian, at Brienne's side, had also fallen asleep. Two of the other adult leaders, Ray and Cameron, were out of the room sharing coffee and conversation. Mary

Hannah Pray and Kelly Gianna Godfrey, two very young female volunteers, were in the kitchen snacking and talking and sharing humor with each other. Suddenly Katrina, lying on her back, shot right up into a sitting position and looked straight ahead. With that strange jerking motion returning, she rotated her head left and then right. Brienne whispered to her, "Katrina, are you alright?" Katrina did not respond as she laid down again. Brienne did not know what to think of this, but it was beginning to concern her. More disconcerting was what happened a few minutes later. This time, Katrina sat up in her sleeping bag and then attempted to stand while still inside it. She managed to do so by letting the bag fall down around her ankles. She was able, somehow, to step out of her bag and place her feet firmly on the carpeted floor. Without speaking, Katrina slowly began walking through the sleeping youth on the floor and meandered toward the door. Upon reaching the closed doors of the fellowship hall exit, she opened them with some authority as they bounced off their wall protectors. Katrina then walked out, passed Ray and Cameron guarding the door without responding to their greeting, and headed up the steps toward the sanctuary. Brienne got up and walked over to Alex.

"Alex," she said. "Katrina has been acting very strange this evening. You saw her leave the room. She seems like she is in some sort of trance."

"Why don't you follow her and see if she's all right," responded Alex as he wondered if he should go as well, due to what had transpired earlier in the day. He was, however, the only adult who was awake in the undercroft and someone had to be watching to make sure things were in good order while chaperoning the youth. This, of course, was his primary responsibility. It was one he took very seriously.

Brienne went quietly through the double doors and asked Ray and Cameron, who were sitting at a table near the entrance of the hall, which direction Katrina had gone. They informed Brienne that when they addressed Katrina, she did not respond. They thought it odd, though they did not pursue it. Informing Brienne that Katrina had headed for the stairwell and ascended the steps, she went quickly upstairs as well. Entering the nearly dark sanctuary, there stood Katrina standing behind the altar with her hands resting upon it. Once again Katrina was expressionless and was staring out into space. Brienne approached her saying, "Katrina, what are you doing? Are you alright?"

Katrina did not answer and did not move. Brienne was now unnerved by Katrina's behavior and so she approached her slowly. "Katrina, Katrina, why aren't you answering me?" asked Brienne. Reaching out, Brienne put her hand on Katrina's right shoulder. Immediately, Katrina's head rotated in the jerking motion that Brienne had noticed previously. She looked at Brienne and then produced a rather chilling smile on her face. Brienne removed her hand and began stepping backward away from Katrina. Failing to pay attention to her location on the chancel, Brienne took one step too far, lost her balance, fell backward, and landed on her back on the risers with her head hitting hard on the floor of the nave. Her fall make quite a thumping sound. Ray and Cameron, still sitting outside the fellowship hall, heard the sound and came running up the stairs. They were followed by Hannah and Kelly who also heard it from their location in the kitchen. There, they saw Brienne lying on the floor unconscious with Katrina at the top of the chancel steps staring down at her. One of the men ran to the undercroft to get Ian and Alex. The other one bent over Brienne and cradled her head in his hands. All this time Katrina made no motion and spoke no words.

"What's wrong with you, Katrina? Get down here and help me. Brienne might have a concussion and we might have to get her to the emergency room," stated Ray.

Just then Ian and Alex ran into the sanctuary with Cameron following them. Ian bent down and over Brienne taking her limp body in his hands and placing her head on his lap. Speaking to her and touching her face, Ian tried to get her to respond. Alex, for his part, moved directly to Katrina. He placed his hands on her upper arms just below her shoulders and shook her. "Katrina, what is wrong with you. Snap out of it! Snap out of it, I say." Just then Katrina went limp and fell into Alex's torso. Alex caught her and laid her down on the floor with her head resting on his lap. At this point, Katrina came to and looked up at Alex.

"What happened? Where am I?" Katrina inquired.

"You are in the sanctuary. Do you know what happened to Brienne?" asked Alex.

"Brienne?" answered Katrina in the form of an inquiry.

"Yes, Brienne – she is lying here unconscious. What happened? What in God's name went on up here?" asked Alex hurriedly.

"I don't know," replied Katrina. "How did I get up here?"

"Hey Alex," cried Ian excitedly. "Brienne is beginning to come to!"

"Gee, I must have been sleepwalking. I don't remember a thing," continued Katrina.

Just then, Brienne began moving. Her eyes opened up and a look of pain appeared on her face. She began rubbing her head with her hands. Ian, Alex, Ray, Cameron, and the two female volunteers expressed a sigh of relief as she moved her legs. There appeared to be no spinal injury and she appeared to know everyone who continued to bend low over her.

"What happened, Brienne?" asked Alex first.

As Brienne stood up and took a seat on the front pew on the Gospel Ambo side of the church she said, "Katrina was acting strange in the fellowship hall. When she got up and left the room, I followed her as you know. I found her standing, seemingly mesmerized behind the altar. She did not speak to me or move. I walked over beside her, and then reached out my hand toward her. When I touched her shoulder, she turned her head and gave me a rather strange smile that was sort of evil looking. It caused me to back up, and not paying attention, I stepped off the chancel, lost my balance, and fell backward."

'I don't remember any of that," replied Katrina with an amazed expression on her face. "Oh my, what is going on with me anyway? Yes, I must have been sleepwalking. That's it – that's the answer. I am sorry, Brienne, that I put you through this and that I precipitated your fall."

"Have you ever been known to have walked in your sleep before?" questioned Alex.

"No, I do not recall ever having that happen to me before," replied Katrina.

"Ian, you had better take Brienne to get her examined," pronounced Alex.

"I'm ok, really I am," stated Brienne. "I'm just going to probably get a bad headache out of this."

"Regardless," stated Ian, "I am going to take you to be examined after this event is over whether you want to go or not."

With that, Ian, Brienne, Ray, and Cameron left the sanctuary and went back down into the fellowship hall as no one was currently present with the group. Hannah and Kelly followed them as well. Katrina was still resting her head on Alex's lap. Alex then said, "Do you think that the experience you had this afternoon had anything to do with this event tonight?"

"I don't know," stated Katrina.

"In the morning, I plan to have a talk with Hugh. You need to be watched," stated Alex. "If any more of this kind of stuff happens, I want you to tell me about it immediately. Please don't hide anything from me. This is a bit disconcerting, and your husband certainly needs to know about it."

"Yes, I will contact you if anything strange happens to me," agreed Katrina. "Please, whatever you do, do not make it a big issue with my husband. He is very protective, and I do not want him to get weirded out by this episode."

At that point, Katrina and Alex returned to the undercroft. The sleepover continued without any further incident or disruption. All the adults remained awake throughout the rest of the night. Ray and Cameron continued their coffee drinking binge and entertained themselves with their own unique humor. Brienne and Katrina kept a close eye on each other. Kelly took the opportunity to spend time in conversation with Ian. She was actually hanging all over him. She was secretly infatuated with him and was very happy to catch him alone while Brienne was distracted. Her objective was to try to get Ian to notice her, and perhaps to go out with her instead of Brienne. Hannah left early and drove home. Brienne did get medical attention later that morning. Fortunately, she did not suffer a concussion. Alex, however, was a bit unnerved by the circumstances reported to him about his lifelong friend. He did share in a telephone conversation with Hugh later in the morning about his wife's behavior that night, but he did not mention anything about the uneasiness he felt within his soul about her condition spiritually. He hoped that this episode was nothing, but he certainly feared that something very malicious was beginning to raise its ugly head. Placing a telephone call to Father Dave of Holy Trinity Church in Saxonburg now became more of a priority on his agenda as Christmas Eve and Day were almost upon them.

Stave 4

A Spooky Little Girl Like You

aving slept very little at the Middle School Youth Group sleepover, Katrina fought to stay awake throughout most of the day on Saturday. It was the Saturday before Christmas and she had a great deal of holiday preparations to make for her husband, her daughter, and their extended family. She and Hugh were hosting Christmas dinner for everyone, and both sets of grandparents wanted to spend the day with Moriah. Moriah was just five years old, so this would be a very special holiday for her. Katrina went to bed exhausted at sunset. Hugh, who made dinner for the trio, was cleaning up the kitchen. Only five minutes passed after Katrina hit the pillow before she was fast asleep. This "long winter's nap" was not going to pass peacefully. Around eight in the evening, Hugh was preparing Moriah for bedtime. Suddenly he heard the loudest scream he had ever witnessed coming from his wife in the bedroom. The screams continued as he hastened towards her. He burst through the door, turned on the light, and found Katrina sitting up in bed still screaming at the top of her voice. Launching himself onto the mattress, he took his wife in his arms and tried to comfort her. Sobbing uncontrollably, Katrina was unable to speak. Hugh positioned his face opposite hers and said, "Honey, what is the matter? Why are you screaming? What has upset you so?"

Katrina reached out and wrapped her arms around Hugh and clung to him tightly. Her warm tears flowed onto and down his neck. She was shaking violently. Hugh broke the embrace and placed his hands on her cheeks. He directed her gaze to his face and spoke to her. "Look at me – look at me. Calm down, you are safe with me. Just calm down – everything is all right now. Compose yourself and find your voice. Tell me why you are screaming. Tell me what happened to make you react like this."

"I – I – I d-d-don't know. I – I – I h-h-had a b-b-bad dream. No, it-it-it was a nightmare – the worst n-n-nightmare I have ever had. It was awful, Hugh," she said as she embraced him once more. "Hold me tight, my love, it was all too-too-too terrible – it seemed so-so-so real. I have n-n-never h-h-had a nightmare like this one in my whole l-l-life. You do love me, Hugh, don't you?"

"Yes, I do Kat," stated Hugh. "I love you very much with all my heart and soul. Why would you ask that?"

"B-b-because in my dream we were separated and I w-w-was all alone."

"That's weird," stated her husband. Hugh then spied Moriah at the door with an expression of fear on her face. "Let me take care of Moriah and make sure she is ok. Then I want you to tell me all about your nightmare."

Hugh turned and stood up. He quickly scooped up Moriah in the doorway and said, "Everything's fine, my darling. Your mother just had a very bad dream. That's all! It's time for bed now!"

Moriah clung to her father with her little arms around his neck as he carried her into her bedroom. "Daddy, could you please leave a light on?" she implored.

"Certainly, I can," stated Hugh with love and care in his voice.

Hugh then read her a short bedtime story and tucked her in, leaving a small bedstand light on. As he said "goodnight" and left the room, he did not close the door the entire way. However, he didn't want his daughter to hear what her mother was about to tell him.

Hugh said to Katrina, "Let's go downstairs into the living room to talk about your nightmare."

Katrina agreed as they walked hand in hand down the steps. Hugh made sure he left the upstairs hallway light on for his daughter's comfort. Once downstairs, Hugh brought her a glass of water and sat beside her on the couch. He said, "Ok Kat, tell me what upset you so."

"Well, my nightmare appeared to be waterborne," stated Katrina. "I was lying on my back in a great lake of water. I was all alone. The lake was motionless. There were no waves. There was also no land in sight. I became perplexed as to how I had gotten there and what I was going to do to get out of there. The lake appeared to be bottomless. By that, I mean I couldn't see or touch the lake bed with my feet. I started to panic knowing that I would eventually tire out from treading water. Even lying on my back was no good because without moving my arms and legs I found that I would start to sink. Then, from far away, I heard and then I saw a great commotion in the water. Something huge and disturbing was coming my way travelling fast and just below the surface. It was pushing up a great mound of water and spraying it high in the air. When it got to me it swirled around and around me several times. Then all of a sudden it stopped. The water calmed. What appeared to be the head of a great monster – just the top – surfaced out of the sea. It was green and scaly. Two large dark eyes opened and looked right at me for what seemed to be the longest time. It appeared to me that it was looking right through me like it knew me or was studying everything about me. As it continued peering into my soul, I sensed the beast's complete disgust and hatred for me. Then, all of a sudden, it raised its long neck, rolled over, and submerged again. The beast resurfaced and again circled around me. The sea monster - that's the best way I can describe it - rose way up from the water, opened its large cavernous dark mouth with sharp bristling yellow teeth and clutched me within its jaws. I was horrified, but it did not clamp down on me. Its teeth were razor sharp and the tips of it cut me as my blood trickled into its mouth. It was moving fast on top of the water, taking me away. Then, I saw what appeared to be land – actually an island. The monster was now hovering above the water like a dragon and then it spit me from its mouth onto the shore. Immediately, the monster disappeared as if into thin air. I was drenched in blood but still alive and able to get up and move. The island was tiny and barren. There was nothing on it but weird things. I saw a sled. I saw an old rusty turned over car. There was part of an old-time paddlewheel boat on it. There was also a deteriorating train engine buried in its yellowy-brown soil. There was a pile of big black rocks and some sort of white stuff all over part of the ground. Also, there was this overturned big black pot or kettle. I didn't know what this stuff meant or why it was there. There was also this fire burning at the top of a mound. It was very hot and produced a lot of black smoke which reached high into the air. All of a sudden, the smoke turned white. Rising from the fire was a gray shadowy figure. It took the form of a person – a ghostly shape. I could make out its contours but still see through it. It grew larger and larger and formed a hideous face. It bent my way as I was on my knees before the fire. It then moved up into the air and hovered over me. I was terrified. What frightened me the most was the moment its face changed into my face. There I was a figure in the smoke looking down upon myself face-to-face. I saw myself both ways at the same time. It was so weird! My face in the fumes then started laughing and laughing at me as blood poured out from the eyes of my smoky countenance. The blood did not just pour out – it sprayed out! It sprayed out all over me. I was bleeding out on myself! That's when I started screaming in my dream and for real. I was absolutely terrified." At this juncture, Katrina leaned into her husband. "What do you think it all means, Hugh?" asked Katrina.

"I don't quite know what to make of it, Kat," answered Hugh. He tried to understand if it had any meaning at all or if there was a hidden message in it. "Let me reflect on it awhile. It sure was rich in symbolism, come to think of it. This might be one for a shrink to try to decipher."

Katrina and Hugh spent almost an hour trying to make some sense of the dream. Katrina stayed up late that night. She was too disturbed to sleep. Eventually, she fell asleep in her husband's arms. It was not the end of the nocturnal horrors for either of them that night.

Deep into the night, Hugh, who was now sleeping beside his wife, felt a tug to the blankets. They were now sliding across his body and lifting into the air. He thought that Katrina by rolling over had captured all the blankets. He turned over on his back to spy a chilling sight. There, above the bed, Katrina had levitated upward about three or four feet and was suspended in the air. Immediately, Hugh jumped out of bed, turned on the light, and stared at his wife. He could not believe what he was seeing. Was he having a nightmare too? He started to reach out his arms to put one on top of Katrina and the other under her to guide her back down onto the mattress, when she turned her head toward him. At first, she had a devilish smile on her face. She then opened her mouth wide to reveal nothing but darkness inside. Katrina stared at him with an evil gaze that he had never seen on her before. At this he backed a couple of steps away. Slowly, with her eyes still fixed on him, she turned with her legs and feet downward. She seemed to be getting out of bed to prepare to walk on the floor. Hugh continued stepping backwards toward the bedroom door. Katrina floated downward to the doorway. With outstretched arms, like portrayals of the Frankenstein monster, she advanced toward her husband. Hugh heard a shrill shriek behind him. It was Moriah, holding her teddy bear. She was horrified at the sight of her floating mother. At the sound of the scream, Katrina's body jerked and immediately fell to the floor. Hugh looked at his wife, then at his daughter. He grabbed Moriah to comfort her. "Moriah, I've got to check on your mommy. Please go into your room and stay there until I call you, ok?" He then went to his wife, got down on his knees, and turned her over.

Katrina looked up at him. The wicked look on her face was gone. "What's going on, Hugh?" she asked. "Why am I out here on the floor of the hallway? How did I get here? I don't have any memory of leaving the bed?

"Honey, I hate to tell you this," said Hugh, "but I found you levitating above our bed. Then you went vertical and began floating after me as I left the bedroom and entered the hallway. Moriah saw you and screamed. At that instant you fell to the floor and woke up. Are you hurt? Are you able to stand?"

It appeared that she had sprained both her ankles. Katrina found it difficult to walk and she was in some pain.

Thinking of her daughter, Katrina said, "Moriah saw me in that condition – oh no, dear Jesus, please help us!"

"Kat," said Hugh, we've got to get you looked at. Perhaps we need to get you examined both medically and psychologically. We also need to see Alex as soon as the church's morning services are over. If he is available, we need to make an appointment with him for this afternoon. We really need to see him right away - I'm sure of it. Something awful is going on here with you and we need to get to the bottom of it fast. I think we should start with Alex in seeking professional help. I'll get on the phone later this morning and make arrangements with your mother to watch Moriah. Let's see how your ankles feel before we attempt to see a doctor. Meanwhile, how about taking a hot bath? It might help to soak those ankles. What do you think? Is it ice or heat on them? I can't remember. Katrina told Hugh the correct treatment. She was terribly afraid to fall back asleep. She fortified herself with "hi-test" coffee and so awaited the dawning of the new day.

Stave 5

Boara's Curse

ittle did Alex and Katrina know that their relationship was more than just a friendship. As they were about to find out, the two of them were linked together through a common ancestor.

Literature portrays many infamous witches in European and American culture. Perhaps the most eminent are the three witches in Shakespeare's *MacBeth*; the "Wicked Witch of the West" in *The Wizard of Oz* - made famous by Margaret

Hamilton; the queen witch in the fairy tale of *Snow White;* and the cannibal witch in *Hansel and Gretel.* Witches abound in American media, such as the popular television show *Bewitched.* The macabre story of a Scottish country witch, named Boara Samus Nevanthi, did not make it into the story books or the pages of history. She practiced her sorcery in the Glen Shee area of Perthshire, Scotland. Glen Shee is known as the "glen of the fairies" in times long past. Today a portion of the Glen Shee area is part of the Cairngorms National Park. Of note to the reader is that William Shakespeare mentions the Great Birnam Wood and Dunsinane Hill in Perthshire as a part of the setting for *Macbeth.* It is in this setting, in the same general area, that the great Bard focuses the prophecy of fate and destiny conjured forth by the three witches in his play. This area was a known haunt of witchcraft to none other than King James VI of Scotland, who later became known as King James I of England. King James was very interested in eliminating the foul presence of the occult from this region.

Boara practiced her sorcery and magic arts outdoors over a wilderness fire. From the flames and smoke she created, she called forth spirits to do the bidding of her clients. Seeking her out in the forest, her customers paid her well to bring them good fortune often at the expense of others, or to conjure up a cursed spirit to exercise calamity and to bring tragedy upon their enemies. Dark shadowy figures would rise out of the fire during her incantations and quickly fly off to perform their ruinous deeds.

Boara became quite wealthy due to her occult enterprise. Her trade in mystic practices gained her both popularity and derision. She lived in the village of Spittal. Here she attempted to convey to onlookers nothing more than the pursuit of a regular life. She was, however, anything but a normal subject of the Crown. Too many people grew jealous due to her growing wealth. They openly wondered how she procured her substance. Too many people believed that there was something dark and foreboding about her. People came to fear her. Too many people had fallen in Perthshire due to the diabolical spells she cast. Rumors began to spread like wildfire identifying her as the evil witch of the Glen Shee forest. Something had to be done with her before the ruination of many a good person in the shire

Donald MacKenzie was a farmer in the Perthshire region. He was also a leading member of the nearby village which he called home. Donald, among others, believed that a curse had come down upon him and some of his neighbors. Their cows had all become instantly sick and died. While superstition reigned supreme in these days, the truth was that Boara had been paid handsomely to pronounce a curse upon the cattle of this village. It was done in order to make the cattle of a local nobleman more valuable and lucrative in trade. Donald and his fellow farmers had no evidence for this other than hearsay. That, however, was enough for them. A group of them made a pact with each other to eliminate the witch, permanently ridding themselves forever of her foul presence. Conducting nighttime forays in the area and bribing those whom they believed might have been her patrons, they discovered the location of her vile practice. In a midnight raid they closed in quietly and slowly surrounded her. The men spied several gray figures come forth from the fire at her command, and in a swirling motion begin to fly off in various directions. It became too much for Donald MacKenzie to idly stand by and tolerate. He signaled the attack as a dozen men rushed in from all sides. Donald himself carried a bucket of water to throw on the fire, but he inadvertently hit Boara instead. Dowsed with water, her long black hair fell flat against her torso as a white vapor steamed off her essence. She then pointed at Donald and pronounced a curse upon him. Donald heard her speak clearly. She cursed one female member of his descendants in each generation to meet a tragic end by dying in a watery accident. Once pronounced, Donald produced his claymore and heaved the heavy sword to strike her down. Instead, Boara stepped into her fire and she looked up into the dark sky with upraised arms as she uttered a great laugh. She then began twirling in circles to the amazement of all the onlookers. They were absolutely mesmerized and frozen in place by the action occurring right in front of them. The next thing they knew she simply disappeared before their eyes while producing a great puff of gray smoke. Nothing of her remained. There was no trace of her anywhere.

In the aftermath of her disappearance, the items of her occult practice were destroyed. Her household possessions and coinage were either stolen by the unscrupulous or distributed to those individuals and families the villagers believed she had cursed. Her ramshackle house was considered vile and thus it was burned down to the ground. The land was then salted. It is said that the lot is still vacant to this very day.

Donald MacKenzie was married to Elizabeth McKay. They only had one child, a daughter, whom they named Sarah. Sarah grew up, married a man named John Robert Hyndman. She bore him ten children before she met a tragic end. One day, while making soap, the large black kettle she was using to perform this chore unexplainably fell from the fire, turned over toward her, poured out its contents upon her, and scalded her to death. She was the first victim in a series of tragic events. In each generation, right up to the present day, one or more females from the MacKenzie lineage suffered strange deaths borne by water.

Immediately after the Sunday morning service of the Church of the Transfiguration had ended, Hugh Helman began telephoning Father McKenzie. He made contact with him on his third attempt. Explaining to Alex about the previous night, the two agreed to meet, along with Katrina, early in the afternoon.

At 1:30 PM, Alex greeted Hugh and Katrina as they entered the church and proceeded to his office to talk. Hugh and Katrina explained in great detail the account of the previous day and night. As they shared what had transpired in their home, something Katrina stated caught Alex's ear. Katrina mentioned in passing a curse on her family. At that, Alex halted the progress of her speech and asked, "Katrina, what curse? What are you talking about? You never, in our whole lives, ever mentioned some sort of curse on your family. Please explain – tell me about it, please!"

"Well, whether you know it or not, I am part Scottish even though much of my family comes from eastern Europe," stated Katrina.

"Katrina," jocularly replied Alex, "since your maiden name is McLaren, that is a dead giveaway that you have some Scottish blood in you. We may have never discussed it, but it is all too obvious for me not to have figured that one out, my friend."

"Oh, yeah, I guess that would be obvious to you." answered Katrina. She continued, "Coming down the Scottish line of the family is a story about a witch who placed a curse on us. My grandmother informed me that one person in the family would meet a tragic end in each and every generation. I never paid much attention to the story because I thought it was just a nonsensical legend passed down from the old country."

"Can you tell me more?" asked Alex.

"Well, my grandmother said that it would be a death that had something to do with water and that the curse was on female members of the family," stated Katrina.

"Do you know of any female members of the family that met tragic ends in or around water?" asked Alex.

"Well, yes, come to think of it, I do. Reflecting on family history, there is a long line of accidental and strange deaths going way back in my family," stated Katrina with a sense of fear rising in her heart. "My aunt Maude died during a rain storm when a hillside gave way and pushed her car off a road along the Allegheny river and down into the water. She drowned. Before that I had a relative named Mary Kay. She was my great aunt. One day, as a young girl, she was swimming in a river. A lot of the guys she was swimming with liked to challenge each other to dive under the boats at that time – paddle wheelers – and come out the other side. Only she didn't make it. The paddle wheeler got her. Before that, I had relatives in the family line– Tom and Charlotte were their names. They liked to go caving. 'Spelunking', I think you call it. I was told that she had an accident on one of their adventures, when the rock roof collapsed and trapped her in the cave. Tom escaped. When the men who helped Tom dig her out, they discovered that the water had risen and drowned her. Prior to that, another relative, her name was Viola, was walking the railroad tracks somewhere. As she was crossing a bridge, a train came and it hit her, knocking her into the river below. She died as well. Then I was told that I had a relative named Twyla. She was coming down a steep hill on a bobsled – I don't know if this was in Scotland or America. The bobsled went out of control, hit a bridge abutment, and threw her and others into an icy river. I was told she and a boy lost their lives. I don't remember any others except for the story of my great, great, great, great, great – grandmother from back in Scotland.

"Wow, that goes back – let me count them – five, six, maybe seven generations," offered Alex. "What happened in your great – however many it is – grandmother's story from back in Scotland?" asked Alex.

"Her name was Sarah Hyndman. The story goes that she was making soap one day and the kettle overturned and scalded her to death," responded Katrina.

"Whoa," stated Alex as he stopped Katrina from speaking any further. "Did you say that your ancestor's name was Sarah Hyndman?"

"Yes, I did," replied Katrina.

"That's weird," stated Alex pondering out loud. "I had an ancestor named Sarah who died in Scotland while making soap. She was scalded to death as well. Do you suppose we are talking about the same person? Was 'Hyndman' your ancestor's maiden or married name?"

"If I am correct, I think it was her married name," stated Katrina.

"Do you know her maiden name?" he asked Katrina.

"No, not offhand," she replied.

"It was MacKenzie. She was Sarah MacKenzie Hyndman," stated Alex. "I think you and I are very distant relatives."

"Wow, no wonder we've always had a connection with each other all these years," said Katrina with a twinkle in her eye.

"I've never heard anything about a curse though," mused Alex. "What do you know about this curse?"

"All I was told by my grandmother is that a witch in Scotland put this curse on the family. My grandmother is deceased so I can't get any more information from her. I will have to ask my mother if she knows anything," replied Katrina. "I do know that the witch's name was Boara. I don't know anything else."

"Katrina, has anyone in your family or extended family – a female, of course, in your current generation met a tragic end in or around water?" asked Alex.

"No, not that I know of," replied Katrina.

"You know, if this curse is real and still active, you, your sister, or cousins could be targeted. And I hate to bring this up, but what about Moriah?" Alex stated.

"Oh, good Lord, I never thought about me or Moriah," exclaimed Katrina. "Alex, what about your daughter, Kendall? What if she could be targeted in this curse since you are a descendant from Sarah MacKenzie as well?" questioned Katrina.

"That does present us with some urgency in this situation. We not only have a peculiar situation going on with you, but potentially a curse to rid ourselves of as well," stated an alarmed Alex.

"You know, since Katrina's nightmare on Saturday night was waterborne and the symbolism was quite intriguing, I have to think that you and Moriah might just be the next targets of the curse. Think for a minute – a foul phantom coming out of a fire with all those symbols of death on that little island: the sled; parts from a river boat paddle wheeler; a partially buried old train engine; a rusted out old automobile; an old black kettle; and some rocks. I wonder if the white material you mentioned poured out upon the ground was soap. All of these things are a link to Sarah and the curse. Either your subconscious is trying to tell you something, or your dream was placed there on purpose by an evil entity. This is weird, but what if your ancestors are calling out to you and trying to warn you of a very clear and present danger?" Thinking for a moment, Alex continued, "Wow, I know that what I just mentioned is an extremely strange thought that might be way out there. You know another thing that bothers me about your dream is that the shadowy gray figure formed by the smoke over the fire – the one which ended up being your face staring right back at you. Other than the fact that this symbolism was used in one of the Star Wars movies, which could have meant two or three things, I wonder if your dream has any connection with the haunting you experienced when Jimmy Mack and Audrey were here on Friday? You said that the phantom dove on you, went right through you, and disappeared. What if – and this is just conjecture on my part right now – it didn't leave you, but has attached itself to you? That would explain a lot of things. Obviously, if what I am telling you is true, it knows about the curse. And if it knows about the curse, it may, heaven forbid, enact it upon you - and soon! Whatever is possessing you might just initiate that awful curse," Alex repeated as the possible horror of it all sank into his consciousness. "Maybe that is what is going on here."

"'Possession'! 'Possession'! Alex, you used the word 'possession'. I am a Christian. Jesus is my Lord and Savior.

I didn't think Christians could be possessed by a demon," stated a frightened Katrina.

"'Possession' may be the wrong word to use. A better word might be 'oppression.' You might be under some sort of demonic oppression. From what I understand, Christians can certainly be oppressed. But I am not an expert on this kind of stuff. I am not even certain if possession, by that I mean a total or a complete takeover of one's person, is even possible. Again, I just don't know," said Alex. "I need to make a call to Father Dave at Holy Trinity. I wonder if I can catch him later this afternoon or this evening. I am glad we do not have youth group tonight! One more thing, Katrina, I want to look up on the internet the name of the witch. Her first name is Boara. Do you know how to spell it – is it 'B-O-R-E-A' or 'B-O-R-A'?" asked Alex.

"It is neither of those" replied Katrina. I think it is spelled 'B-O-A-R-A'. At least, that is what I remember from my grandmother."

"Are there any other names attached to her? Do you know of any?" asked Alex.

"No, I do not," replied Katrina

"Here we go," as Alex searched around in his computer. Looking under Celtic names, he discovered that "Boara" meant "a flame or purging". What Alex and Katrina did not know was that Boara possessed a middle name. This name was "Samus", which means "one who supplants". Her last name was also unknown to them. It was "Neventhi", which refers to a "spiritual or holy lady."

"Katrina, do you have to work tonight or tomorrow?" asked Alex.

"I am not scheduled to work again until Tuesday," said Katrina.

"Good," announced Alex. "Hugh, take Katrina home and don't let her out of your sight. I will call you immediately after I reach Father Dave."

Alex ushered them out of the church and locked the doors behind him. He immediately proceeded to his study, picked up his office phone, and attempted to contact Father David Freeman at Holy Trinity Church in Saxonburg.

Iceberg Responsibilities

O nce back in his office, Father McKenzie placed a call to Father Freeman of Holy Trinity Church in Saxonburg. Failing to reach him on his office phone, Alex called his cell phone number. This too proved unsatisfactory. Fortunately, he had the cell phone number for Francesca, Father Dave's wife.

"Hello, this is Francesca," she answered.

"Hi, Francesca, this is Father Alex McKenzie from The Church of the Transfiguration in Plum Township. I hope all is well with you. I need to talk to your husband about a matter of some urgency. Is he available to speak?" asked Father McKenzie.

"He's outside right now. Let me see if I can find him. And yes, all is well with both of us. Hold on, Alex," replied Francesca as she left the rectory.

Francesca discovered her husband in the yard setting up some last-minute Christmas decorations. She handed him her device and said to him, "Alex McKenzie is on the phone for you. He says it is important."

"Hi, Alex," stated Father Dave, "What can I do for you today?"

"David, I think I have a pretty unusual and fairly bad case of what appears to be demonic oppression or possession on my hands here. I am not well-versed in handling this kind of situation. I need your help. I was hoping I could explain the situation to you, and then you could advise me on what steps to take next. It is no secret that you, and your church, were involved with some sort of demonic activity a few years ago," stated Alex.

"That's right, we had a brief but most frightful occurrence here," acknowledged Father Dave. "Let me head inside the house and then you can explain to me what you are encountering."

Alex explained in great detail what he was experiencing with Katrina and the circumstances inside the church at the sleepover. Father Dave, unfortunately, could not be much help. He knew little of the real situation in his own church, and nothing about how the demonic presence was eradicated.

He said to Alex, "How well do you know Father Jeff at the Church of the Incarnation in Natrona Heights?"

"Not very well, I am afraid, but of course I have met him,' stated Alex.

David went on to say, "Give him a call. Just a few days ago he had an issue with what appeared to be a demonic entity at his church. We belong to the same clergy prayer and support group. The story he told was pretty amazing, and I am sure he did not share everything with us."

"Ok, I'll get in touch with him right away. Thank you for your help, and may you and your wife have a great Christmas," stated Alex joyfully.

"You too, Alex, and may God be present with you on this one," replied Father Dave.

Alex then attempted to get Father Fairlamb on the phone. There was no answer and so he left a message for Jeff to call him immediately. Alex decided to retire to his house. It was now past mid-afternoon and his wife Annalena was probably wondering what was delaying him from coming home. Sure enough, she was not in the best of moods when he came through the door.

"What kept you from coming home after the service, especially since you do not have youth group meetings tonight?" Annalena inquired.

"Something came up that was important for me to take care of right away," stated Alex.

"What was so important?" asked Annalena. "Tell me what it was this time!"

"Honey, you know that I cannot reveal things told to me in confidence," replied Alex.

"Ok, so who were you with over there?" Annalena inquired.

"If you must know, I was with Katrina. She has a significant problem and this may not be an easy one with which to deal," responded Alex nervously.

"You know, Alex, you spend a lot of time with that woman. I know you've known her almost your entire life. I know that she is one of your best friends. You seem to run to her every time she has a need. It makes me think that the two of you have some sort of thing going on. Sometimes, I think you like her more than me. Sometimes, I think you know her better than you know me. And sometimes, I think you'd prefer being with her rather than me," charged Annalena with more than just a little hurt in her voice.

'Yes, Annalena, I love Katrina, but only as a friend and sister in Christ. You are the one who holds my heart and soul. You have nothing to be jealous of and there is nothing untoward going on between the two of us," remarked Alex with a tender expression to his voice. "In fact, the two of us were not there alone. Hugh was present as well. I can also tell you that I found out today that Katrina and I are related. She possesses some Scottish heritage in her family line, and we were able to trace it back to a common ancestor. This is where it gets strange and potentially serious. Many generations ago a curse was placed on the family by a witch in Scotland, if you can believe that. I know how weird this thing might sound to you, but hear me out. The curse appears to play on one woman in each generation who dies a strange death involving water. The first lady to die was my great, great, great, great something grandmother, Sarah MacKenzie Hyndman. Since that time, one female in Katrina's direct line, more or less, has died a strange death. Nobody in her generation has died yet. I am worried about both Katrina and Moriah coming under the curse if this whole legend is true. I am also worried, since both of us trace our family back to Sarah, that the curse could impact Kendall. This is doubtful, but I am still fearful. Now that we know this, I must help Hugh, Katrina, and Moriah terminate this curse if it is indeed real. Right now, I have to assume it is. Recently over the past couple of days, Katrina's family has experienced some strange and alarming things. The church has also witnessed some peculiar incidents as well. I have already started making phone calls in order to get some help. The visit by Hugh and Katrina, along with the phone calls, has delayed my afternoon return. Please do not be angry with me. You also have nothing to worry about," remarked Alex.

"Alex, you could have at least phoned me," said Annalena.

"You are so right, my dear. Please forgive me," replied Alex.

"Clergy just work too many hours. Your time is not your own and the demands on you are never ending. I love you tremendously and I know that you are a quality priest, but I am having a difficult time dealing with this kind of life. The only consistency to it is that there is no consistency to it at all. Your schedule, and what pops up instantly – unplanned – during the day runs our lives, and, I think, ruins part of our lives." complained Annalena.

"It is called 'iceberg responsibilities,' my dear. My position is not the only occupation with which this term can refer. People see just the tip, like an iceberg, of what is above the water in duties and tasks. They do not know the cumbersome load that is below the water. They also do not account for it. It takes place in many careers. It is just so much worse, it seems, in ministry if you conduct it properly. I have heard from others that some people in the congregation wonder what I do all day. Most church members have no idea. If they did, their attitudes and perceptions might be a little more gracious and understanding. I am always at the mercy of the telephone, e-mail, social media, and those who come through the door," lamented Alex.

Following the conversation, Alex intentionally stopped working for the remainder of the day. He spent his time with Annalena and their young children. His time spent with her, and the words he spoke to her helped to reassure her of his love and fidelity. He truly sympathized with her plight and feelings. He did take her complaint seriously, though he knew it would be a struggle to cut out more time for her and the family. Already he had cut out most of his hobbies and interests, and he socialized very little with his friends. Ministry can often be all-consuming with many things having to be set aside permanently or delayed into the future. The happiness of his wife and their children was important to him. He knew he had to find a way to secure more balance in his life between home and career. He knew that what he was facing would not be easy, and maybe impossible, to accomplish.

On Monday morning, Alex arrived at his office very early. When the time was appropriate, he called Father Fairlamb at the *Church of the Incarnation and the Saints of Advent* in Natrona Heights. Picking up the phone was Jillian Jiganie. "Church of the Incarnation, Jillian speaking," she said.

"Hi, Jillian, this is Father McKenzie - downriver at the Church of the Transfiguration. I'd like to speak to Father Fairlamb if I could please, and where's Verna?" asked Alex.

"Verna is off today. School is out early for the holiday, and so I am filling in for her. I'll transfer the call immediately," Jillian responded.

"Thank you," said Father McKenzie.

Picking up the phone Father Jeff asked, "Hey Alex, how are you doing with Christmas Eve just a couple days away?"

"I am doing fine and I am prepared for all the services and events through the rest of the season. I hear you have quite a schedule, Jeff," commented Alex.

"Yes, I do – that's what I get for celebrating with the church family all these special dates of the saints during this season. It's fun, but it's a great deal of work with a hefty time commitment," observed Jeff. "What can I do for you today?"

"I've got a significant problem here. I've got a possible demonic haunting going on. Father Dave in Saxonburg stated that you had a demonic experience recently, and that you might be able to help me," stated Father McKenzie.

"Yes, we had a very bizarre situation. I never want to go through anything like that again. Explain to me what is happening with you and then I'll share what happened here," offered Jeff. "Honestly, what I will tell you will be very difficult for you to believe!"

Alex then explained the circumstances at the Church of the Transfiguration. After he concluded, Jeff said, "Wow, it sounds like you have a genuine demonic attack upon the person and family you shared with me. Alex, let me now explain what happened to me here. We had a demonic entity take a physical feminine form. The shape she took was of a very – and I mean very – beautiful woman. I know that this sounds crazy, but I am being dead serious – this really happened. I must also inform you, whether you might have heard it or not, that I am recently engaged to Jillian – the woman who answered your call today. She ended up being important in the story I am telling you."

"Congratulations Jeff," exclaimed Alex joyfully.

"This very attractive woman shows up in church and was very forward and enticing. She focused all of her energy on me. I have to admit that I was thinking of breaking it off with Jillian, and dating this woman exclusively. However, I discovered – let's just say with some divine assistance – that this female was the physical manifestation of a demonic entity. I know this must sound crazy to you, but this is no joke. Unfortunately, it was all too real. The demon is known to some as the 'Lady of the Church.' She is no lady. It is an evil fiend who attempts to destroy ministries, churches, and clergy which the 'evil empire' believes are dangerous and destructive to all thing Luciferian. I was able to resist her advances, but she then physically attacked me twice. The last time I suffered a head injury. Jillian, God bless her, had been instructed concerning some things about the deliverance ministry and was able to cast her away from this locale. Alex, what I saw and heard was terrifying and horrific. She was taken down the river by – well let's just say – divine supernatural force. I wonder if the demon that is plaguing you is the same evil entity that attacked us. The time-frame, from what you have told me, fits well."

"What do I do now, Jeff – what do I do?" implored Alex.

"I want you to call the leading exorcist in the Pittsburgh area. I shouldn't call him an exorcist because that means 'to cast out by magic.' There is no magic involved here – it is simply the power of the Christ and God's precious Holy Spirit. The man's name is Doctor James Augustus Remus. I'll have to look up his number and then I'll text it to you. Alex, beware – this demonic entity is nothing to play around with. She is probably not alone either. She must be cast out of your friend, her family, and your church. Don't wait, she can cause a great deal of damage. Call me, please, if you need more information. I'll do what I can to help you, with one exception – I won't be present with you when you confront it. I never want to be in the company of that fiend again. Godspeed and God bless. Let me petition God for you right now over the phone." Father Jeff then delivered a long prayer – especially a prayer of protection for all those involved, including their families. Once the prayer was finished, the two men hung up.

Immediately, Father Jeff looked up Dr. Remus' phone number and forwarded it off to Alex. Alex received it and did not waste any time placing the call. Monday mornings can be a difficult time to reach other people following the weekend, but Dr. Remus answered the phone on Alex's first attempt. "Hello, Jim Remus here!" Dr. Remus' voice was cheerful and friendly. Indeed, he was a super person with a great personality. A strong Christian, he had come to the faith the hard way experiencing much difficulty in life and making many personal errors. Having been previously under attack from supernatural entities, he dedicated his life and ministry to combatting demonic and satanic forces. His life mission, though it was more like a crusade, was to help others who were oppressed and possessed. It was a dark and foreboding ministry, but delivering others from the grip of evil made it all worthwhile.

Alex explained in great detail the circumstances surrounding Katrina, her family, and the church. Tomorrow is the "Eve of the Eve". Fortunately, unlike *The Church of the Incarnation and the Saints of Advent,* he was not officiating a service for the 23rd of December. Dr. Remus agreed to drive up the Allegheny Valley from Pittsburgh and to meet with him, Hugh, and Katrina - if the latter would agree to, and could schedule, a time with him. Jim and Alex opened their schedules to meet with the Helman's any time during Tuesday, day or night. At the end of the conversation, Alex and Dr. Remus engaged themselves in an intense prayer. They pleaded with heaven to respond in some direct way to their situation and to save all those involved in the matter.

Stave 7

Eve of the Eve

Alex placed a call to the Helmans immediately following his conversation with Dr. Remus. With their work schedules, a daytime meeting was not possible. They agreed, however, to come to the church Tuesday night. Alex got the word to Dr. Remus that a 6:30 PM appointment had been arranged. At the appointed hour, the four of them met in the cozy sitting area of the church library. Introductions and small talk dominated the first ten minutes of their time together. Everyone, including Dr. Remus, seemed uncomfortable, anxious, and on edge. Finally, Alex called the quartet to get down to the business at hand. Dr. Remus asked Katrina and Hugh to describe the entire situation. He plied them with many questions. Jim also wanted to make sure that both of them knew Jesus Christ as their Savior and Lord. Once he was satisfied with their responses, and had garnered the information he needed, he led the four of them in prayer.

Dr. Remus invoked Heaven for divine assistance to accomplish the stated purpose of the four individuals gathered there. He also prayed for the protection of the assembled participants, and for God's covering security for their families. Once satisfied with his invocation, Dr. Remus spoke directly to Katrina asking the spirit inside of her to reveal itself. "I am speaking to you, foul entity, what is your name?" cried Jim.

"Excuse me, Dr. Remus," interrupted Katrina with some alarm in her voice, "but I thought that Christians could not be possessed by an evil spirit."

"You may be correct on that my dear, however, this subject has produced a great amount of debate in the Christian community," responded Dr. Remus. "Your situation may appear to be more of a case of oppression than possession, if that makes any sense. Perhaps we will discover which way it is – perhaps not. The curse upon your family is the doorway through which this evil entity has entered, I presume."

"Excuse me again, Dr. Remus," stated Katrina, "must you know the name of the entity to remove it?"

"I want, my dear, to know the kind of entity with which I am dealing. And I want to know if there is more than one of them which has taken up, shall we say, at least a partial residence within you," responded the good doctor.

Again and again, Jim attempted to learn the name of the entity. After several minutes of non-response, Alex was beginning to wonder if there was anything at all attached to Katrina at this time. Then suddenly, it happened. What Alex, Hugh, and Jim noticed was a jerking and ripple effect on Katrina's body. Her frame twisted. Then her arms and shoulders jerked. Her head rotated to the left. Then her head returned facing the three men. A macabre smile broke out on her face. Her eyeballs rolled up inside her head and had disappeared from their sight. All that they could see were the whites of her eyes. And then words came forth from Katrina's mouth in a ghastly and guttural sounding way. Alex had never heard such a tone to the English language before. He was quite perturbed, but remained seated, trusting that Dr. Jim knew what he was doing.

"Tell me, oh foul one, what is your name?" Dr. Jim demanded. "Are you one or many?" he then asked.

Letting out a hideous laugh, Katrina's head snapped backward and then forward again. "We are legion, for we are many. You will never discover us all!"

Boldly speaking up, Alex interjected, "Are you the one they call the Lady of the Church?"

Surprisingly, the demonic entity answered, "Yes, if that is who you think I am and what you want to call me!"

"What is your purpose here? What is your mission?" asked Alex.

"I am what you would call a wrecking entity. My purpose here is to walk this earth and wreak havoc on ministries, destroy churches, and compromise clergy so they falter, fail, and fall. I am here to steal God's own and to bring glory to my master," stated the entity.

"And who is your master?" Alex boldly inquired.

"You know him by many names. I also know that the name Satan strikes great fear in your human hearts," stated the entity, once more laughing.

"You know that you are on the losing side, do you not?" proceeded Alex.

"You may think so, but my master is still looking for and will find that knowledge that will make him equal, if not greater, than the one you have sided with," stated the entity.

"Impossible!" yelled Alex.

"Enough of this line of questioning, Alex," as Dr. Remus reached out to him and grabbed him by the arm, putting pressure on his flesh in order to quiet him. "It is trying to divert us from our primary task. If it, or they, cannot beat us, they will try to outlast us, outfox us, frustrate us, outthink us, outflank us, and tie us up in useless conversation. They will try to do anything to keep us from accomplishing our mission. Even if it, or they, cannot defeat us, they will still try to diminish us in any way possible and attempt to spoil this church. We've got to keep our eyes focused on our primary objective. Enough of this useless conversation."

The entity then laughed again and said, "Try as you will, I can already tell that you three are frightened by my presence. You all secretly desire to run right out of here. Wouldn't you just like to leave and go home and forget the discomfort you feel right now. Go on home and experience peace! Go on home and relax. You do not need this high tension in your lives. Yes indeed, you have every right to be afraid of me. I can cause great harm to all of you – and that includes your little Moriah, Hugh, and your little Kendall, Alex."

At that Alex became exceedingly angry. "I've had enough of this, Dr. Remus. Let's get this foul thing out of her! Jim – Hugh – we can't let this thing remain!" shouted Alex. "The danger and damage it and this curse can wreak upon us is something we cannot fail to challenge and eliminate."

"In the name of Jesus Christ, I demand to know your name," once more asked Jim with authority.

"I have already told you – we are legion," returned the entity.

"You, the voice – the mouthpiece – again in the name of Jesus Christ, whom you cannot resist, what is your name?" asked Dr. Remus pointedly.

With a great hiss and ripple movements evident in Katrina's throat as if something were wiggling up from her interior and entering her mouth, the entity shouted, "Leviathan – I lurk beneath the waves and hover above the waters. I can certainly consume and extinguish all of you!"

At that Alex spoke up and shouted, "I bind you up in the name of…"

Before he could pronounce the name of Jesus, the foul being had a pincer lock on his larynx prohibiting his speech. Gasping for air, Alex was more astonished than he was alarmed. The hold on his neck was very firm and sent him collapsing to his knees from his seated position.

Immediately, Dr. Remus rebuked the evil spirit and Alex's neck was released.

As Alex attempted to catch his breath, the entity employing Katrina's vocal cords laughed once, and then again, as Katrina's head rocked back and forth. Then it addressed Alex, saying, "Your kind are all the same. You think you can fool around with us and defeat us. The three of you need to think better of this situation. I will not let you destroy this curse. In fact, I will magnify the curse to include more people in your family and your precious little Kendall as well. Your kind think you are all so noble and outstanding – high and mighty. You have no idea of the power darkness can wield. Your kind have messed with my kind for too long. You deserve the comeuppance you are going to receive from me. You and yours will not stand in my way anymore. You will not get in the way of my work tonight or in the days to come."

At that, Katrina sat up erect in her chair, and she then began to rise out of it. Then from her mouth she regurgitated a foul stream of vomit in the direction of Alex. Much of it landed on him, covering him with its disgusting and dirty discharge. At this, the completely erect Katrina peered at Alex with a most hateful expression. Then she bent slowly and sat down again. As she did, her body began to contort and collapse in the chair. Katrina then came back into consciousness with the full possession of her faculties. "What is going on here? What just happened?" she asked. "Why do I feel so weird? Have I been asleep or out of it for a while? Why is Alex covered with vomit? Would someone please answer me?" Hugh brought a box of tissues for her mouth. He had been frozen in fear all of this time. He moved quickly toward his wife to give her a tissue. Hugh then placed both of his hands on her shoulders. He stood over her, but was somewhat fearful of embracing her.

"That's it, gentlemen," stated Hugh. "That's enough of this for today! I am pulling the plug on this exercise right now. I don't want to put Katrina through any more trauma this night!"

"I am afraid you are correct, Hugh," stated Dr. Remus with a defeated tone to his voice. "I think we've all had enough this evening. Alex, go take care of yourself."

"Yeah, I will! I will also get a bucket of water, a brush, some towels, and some cleaner to take care of this carpet as well," stated Alex in a matter-of-fact way.

Dr. Remus then described to Katrina what had happened after she lost consciousness. Katrina was absolutely beside herself in hearing Jim's description of the events, as Hugh added his own words of explanation. Hugh drew closer to Katrina, wrapping his arms around her as she focused on Dr. Jim.

"You know, Katrina, we failed today to remove this entity that troubles you. We will have to try again – and this time we must succeed. It is a necessity that we win this battle – you and your family do not want this thing attached to you! You do not want to live with this thing hanging around you! You can't live properly with this thing troubling you! It has got to go, and you have got to cooperate with us until we totally remove it from your person and life." exclaimed Dr. Remus. Jim went on, "Hugh, with what you witnessed tonight you know that I am right. You have got to give me another opportunity here. We have little time to waste."

"I know that you are correct," stated Hugh. "With Christmas Eve tomorrow and Christmas day following that, we are in a calendar quandary. This is a bad time for a holiday in terms of this situation."

At that moment, Alex came back into the room wearing his wet clothing and partially clean clothing. He was, however, more concerned with the carpet than with himself. As he began working on the mess on the floor scrubbing the carpet fibers, Katrina expressed her apologies concerning this blast of her vomit. Alex stated that she need not apologize since it was not her fault. Picking up on the previous conversation heard as he entered the room he stated, "Yes, if everyone agrees, let's get together the day after Christmas. Can we all give assent to do that?"

Everyone agreed with Alex, as both Hugh and Katrina reluctantly nodded their approval.

"Let's go, Kat," said Hugh as he pointed the way to the door.

"I am so sorry, Alex," apologized Katrina, almost in tears. "I am so sorry for causing you all this trouble!"

"We'll get though it – and we'll get through it together," replied Alex.

With that, Hugh and Katrina left the room and walked out of the church.

"Father McKenzie," said Dr. Remus. "We need to spend some time in prayer, just the two of us. Do you realize what that foul entity expressed as its name? Do you know the meaning of the title, 'Leviathan'"?

"Go ahead, please inform me, Jim," responded Alex.

"'Leviathan' means 'twisted and coiled'", stated Dr. Remus. "In antiquity it represented the embodiment of chaos. It was often considered to be the demon of the deadly sin 'envy'. It was believed by some to be the creature that would consume the damned in the afterlife. It is portrayed as a sea serpent – a giant and powerful entity found in the Psalms, Job, Isaiah, Amos, and perhaps, according to some translations, in Jonah. It is also mentioned in the intertestamental book of Enoch. This is no comical 'Beanie and Cecil' type creature. It is said to come out of the sea. The sea was always looked upon as a cauldron of evil, of a maelstrom of churning uncertainty, as a place of death, and from which came evil political schemes. Some believe that 'Leviathan' is represented in the 'Sigil of Baphomet'. In the Old Testament, this being is defeated by Yahweh. It is chilling, however, that this representation keeps coming up again and again in the modern era in terms of demonic attacks upon people. It seems to prey on people and, well, I guess enough said – we do certainly need to pray!"

After Alex finished his work on the carpet, he and Jim sat down and went into a time of intense prayer. They pleaded long and hard with Heaven to come to their aid, and to do so rapidly. Both men expressed confidence that Heaven would help, but Alex secretly possessed some doubt if any divine assistance would be forthcoming. His confidence, both in himself and in God's willingness to help, had been shaken.

Alex was now not only very concerned about Katrina and her family, but also about Kendall as well. There was also no way in which he was going to be able to describe all of these happenings and circumstances to his dear wife. What she did not know, well, would be for the better. This whole thing would freak her out and would spoil the holiday for her and their kids. The magic of the season this particular year, had already been destroyed in his own mind. He had to get through the next two or three days successfully. He reasoned that this might not be so easy to do. How could he express Christmas joy with all of this hanging over him? Yet, the joy of the Christ's victory over death, Hell, sin, and Satan was something he had to proclaim. He also had to believe it, know it, and feel it as he shared the good news with his congregation. It was something he knew he was now called upon to engage in a very personal and timely way. "Maybe now," he reasoned with himself, "Christ's birth has got to mean something incredibly vital and absolutely critical to me in a most personal and direct way."

Stave 8

Third Time's a Charm

eanwhile, Quintas, who was currently in charge of the heaven borne extraordinary prayer response operations for Southwestern Pennsylvania, was being addressed by an under-angel who said to him, "We've got another hot assignment coming down to us from the Cosmic Office. You'll be receiving it telepathically in a moment."

"Thank you for the notice," responded Quintas.

Upon receiving the message, Quintas stated out loud for all in earshot to hear, "Darn it! I just knew it! I knew that the foul demon that was flushed down part of the Allegheny River a few days ago in earth time would be back to trouble us in a jiffy. Get me Feynman ASAP! Tell him to report at once," shouted Quintas to a subordinate. "He fouled up the end of his last mission, and just as I anticipated at that time, we're going to have to send him back to finish the job."

Feynman arrived without hesitation. "Saint Feynman reporting for duty, sir," as he snapped another human oriented military salute to his commanding angel in the best tradition of the heavenly esprit de corps.

"Cut out your earthly expressions of humor. Your comedic performances do not sit too well with me, you know. This is especially true since you botched the end of your last assignment on the planet a few short Earth days ago. I knew that this foul entity would soon be giving us fits again, and that certainly is the case. In fact, your 'Lady of the Church' has its grip on another human being loyal to our Majesty, is prepared to cause havoc at another one of our churches, is trying to neutralize another one of our ministers, and may be preparing to actually kill. All this is occurring due to the fact you didn't finish it off! Are you ready for your next, and what I hope will be on this particular issue, - your last assignment?" asked Quintas.

"Aye, Aye, sir," responded Feynman who stood at attention and proceeded to launch another salute.

"Do you think this is funny, young saint – well do you?" inquired Quintas, who was now completely in an ill mood. "I hope for your sake that 'third time's a charm' as you Earthlings say it. It had better be the end all to this pathetic chapter in your saintly service. I'd like to say to you, 'good luck'. Luck, however, never has anything to do with it, or with us, this time or at any time. Please just follow your instructions and make sure you get these human actors under your influence to do what must be done here. I want this demon – this 'Lady of the Church' as you refer to it, to be permanently disabled and imprisoned. You got that? You had better get it, and get it right this time. In a moment the details of your assignment will be transmitted to you. Well, do you have anything to say for yourself while we wait?"

"Well, yes, I guess I do – it's more like a question though. I have been wondering what kind of name is Quintas?" asked Rasmus Gilbert Feynman of his commanding angel. While I was resident on earth, I heard the names Quinn as in 'Quinn the Eskimo', the actor Anthony Quinn, and that broadcaster guy, Jim 'our leader' Quinn, whose sidekick was known as 'Radio Rose'. I also heard of the names Quentin, Quintin, Quinlan, Quinnell, and Quinta. Come to think of it, there is also an Aussie airline called 'Qantas'. I am also familiar with the name Quintus, spelled with a 'u' instead of an 'a' at the end. I think that is a Latin spelling. Back on Earth, we Americans had a President named, Quincy. I think there was even a television show back several decades ago entitled 'Quincy, M.E.' I even heard of a person people called, Quinty. Since we are becoming such good compatriots, may I refer to you affectionately as Quinty?"

"You certainly may not," snapped Quintas. "Since you, sir, have been around here for a while now, you are beginning to get just a little too comfortable with this place, and with me," exclaimed Quintas.

"The name 'Quintas' on earth means 'small', 'tiny', or 'little'. Certainly, these definitions cannot be used to qualify you, my leader extraordinaire. 'Quintas' can refer to a 'small estate'. In some derivations of the name, it refers to 'intelligence' and 'wise counsel'. That would be true of you, Quintas. It can also mean 'to call up', which is just what you did with me. Furthermore, it can mean 'fifth' as in 'fifth born.' You know, I think that fits you. On Earth, there is a military term known as a 'Fifth Column'. It means a group of soldiers or para-military volunteers who operate to undermine the enemy behind their lines. Fifth Columnists engage in sabotage, disinformation, and espionage – both overt and clandestine. That is what I do on mission, don't you think?" uttered Rasmus.

"I think that you think too much," responded Quintas.

"You also remind me of a James Bond type character," announced Feynman. "Do you know anything about the James Bond series on earth?"

"I don't pay much attention to the drivel you humans produce," stated Quintas.

"In most of the stories about James Bond, there is a character that went by the designation, 'Q'," pronounced Rasmus.

"I guess you're going to tell me anyway, even though I couldn't care less," interrupted Quintas.

Undaunted by the interruption and Quintas' lack of interest, Rasmus continued, "'Q' represents the 'Q' Branch or Division. The Q Branch is the research and development unit of the British Secret Service MI6. MI6 stands for the Military Intelligence, Section 6, I guess. MI6 agents had a license to kill in the Ian Fleming novels and the Broccoli movie series. I guess I have a license to kill, don't I, Quintas? That's exciting for a former earthly priest. This is a real advancement in vocation, don't you think?"

"In this assignment, you certainly do – and it better be accomplished if you know what's good for you!" snapped Quintas.

"I always liked James Bond," announced Feynman.

"Yeah, you and how many other guys around here. This destination is full of them. All of you James Bond devotees were a pretty sinful lot watching, what I can only imagine, are male fantasy spy flicks. You've been forgiven so I guess I can't comment on it anymore," replied Quintas.

Just then the full read-out of the situation at the Church of the Transfiguration on Coxcomb Hill in Plum Township and the Helman residence across the river was fully transmitted to Rasmus. "Wow, this beast gets more vicious with each manifestation. These poor people, they really need our assistance," stated Feynman with a great deal of empathy evident in his voice.

"They most certainly do," uttered Quintas. "By the time we get you through the inter-dimensional transfer portal it will be nighttime on Christmas Eve. We are sending you directly to the church. When you get there, go through the Holy Spirit window high up in the nave. From that vantage spot, do your initial scan for the opposition. Look for any mischievous perturbations the Lady of the Church may have already caused or which she is currently invoking. Take a defensive stand against her. Attempt to protect the worshipping congregation and the sanctity of the service. Following worship, introduce yourself to Father McKenzie when the opportunity is presented to you. Remember, it is Christmas Eve and he may have some late-night responsibilities at home. Your assignment, however, is of primary importance. Father McKenzie must understand that, regardless of any intention he might have of portraying Saint Nicholas late at night for his children. Make sure that he realizes that 'the main thing is to make sure the main thing is the main thing'. You make that very clear to him. Do you understand?"

"Yes, sir," responded Feynman without repeating any of his ghostly soldier style salutes.

"Good," replied Quintas, "and one more thing…."

"I know," interrupted Rasmus, "I am not permitted to reveal myself to friends and family."

"That is correct, my saint," barked Quintas. "Now off with you, and do not disappoint me!"

Stave 9

Christmas Eve Debacle

It was Christmas Eve, a time when Alex ought to have been excited, joyous, and expectant of good things to come his way, not only for himself, but also for the church. He was, however, full of anxiety and foreboding. He actually feared the coming hour of the highly celebrative and traditional Christmas Eve service. He was most apprehensive about the evening, considering the fact that the Lady of the Church had not been exorcized from Katrina or even the premises. Openly, he wondered to himself if it would be wise for Hugh, Katrina, and Moriah to be in attendance. While he had not suggested to Hugh and Katrina that they stay away from the church that evening, he secretly hoped that they would come to that conclusion and stay home. The fact of the matter was that both Hugh and Katrina were afraid to appear in church that night, for the entity within her might make a demonstration of itself for all to see. The couple decided that it would be best for all concerned if they did not attend, or go anywhere else on this particular evening. So they stayed home. They reasoned that there was plenty they could do to make it a memorable evening for Moriah. They did not, however, communicate their coming absence to Alex, which left him filled with trepidation.

Alex and Ian would officiate the service from the chancel area, Alex on the Gospel Ambo side and Ian on the Epistle Ambo side. Kelly Gianna Godfrey would be helping Ian with the children's message, as she took great interest in so doing. Together, she and Ian had a very special message for the children and an ornamental gift for each of them to place on their tree at home. Kelly and Ian worked well with each other. They took great delight in their mutual ministry, much to the growing concern of Brienne. Mary Hannah Pray was in charge of all the acolytes and candle-passers that evening. Kelly and Hannah would be sitting up front on the Epistle Ambo side of the nave with some of the children involved in the evening's service. Ray and Cameron had volunteered to handle ushering duties. They hung out in the rear of the church drinking coffee, as usual, and finding much humor in the evening as they greeted, escorted, and observed the worshippers.

Rasmus Gilbert Feynman arrived through the Holy Spirit window. This window in the Church of the Transfiguration was located on the eastern face of the building. It was designed to allow the rising sun to bathe the sanctuary in the bright light of the new day during certain times of the year. Of course, on Christmas Eve no natural light would be penetrating the window from outside. Here Rasmus came to rest after his inter-dimensional journey.

Everything initially went well with the service. Before and after the processional, Alex scanned the full house to see who was, or who was not, present, including the Helmans. He was a bit relieved when he discovered that they were probably not in the house. Just as Alex breathed a sigh of relief, however, the shenanigans began. While the Helmans were not in attendance, the Lady of the Church was about to make her presence known. She had detached herself from Katrina for the purpose of paying a little visit on the worshipping congregation.

Her entry was dramatic. She blew open the front doors of the church in a sudden motion which allowed a cold rush of air, of her own making, to blow right down the center aisle, extinguishing all the pew candles. Ray and Cameron, almost in a panic, quickly rushed to the doors and, pushing hard against the column of air opposing them managed to close them. Both men looked in the direction of Alex and raised their arms, extended their hands, and shrugged their shoulders signaling their confusion as to the circumstances which surrounded this great rush of air.

Feynman, from his perch high above the sanctuary, quickly realized that he was witnessing the work of his primary nemesis. Rasmus reasoned that he should make a demonstration to this foul entity that he was now present in the church that night. His hope was that if she knew he was there, that it might quench her vile machinations and end her plans to spoil the service. Totally invisible to the worshipping congregation, he swept down and over the aisle candelabrum. As he flew by, the candle fire returned to each and every candlestick much to the amazement of the congregation. Oohs and ahhs went up from all the people in the pews, as this became an initial indication that possibly the evening would portray a night of miracles. The extraordinary re-lighting permeated the hearts and minds of many of the worshippers with a sense of mystery and expectation. For their part, Alex and Ian stared at each other across the expansive chancel area, not sure what to make of the strange occurrence. It certainly, however, put the two of them on edge.

Rasmus, unfortunately, had miscalculated. The devious demon, realizing that she was not alone and had an adversary in the building, decided not to cease and desist, but to press forward with her wicked designs. The Lady of the Church had noticed that the ceiling fans were off and had not been on for a long time. A great build-up of dust had accumulated on the blades. In actuality, the electrical switch controlling the fans was broken and had not been repaired. No one had bothered to clean the blades as well. They were, after all, attached to the ceiling and were quite high. Laughing to herself, the vile fiend manipulated the malfunctioning electrical switch and provided the spark to turn them on. Slowly at first, and then faster and faster, the blades whirled around at high-speed, covering the entire congregation in dust as it fell from the ceiling. Now the oohs and ahhs of the congregation turned to choruses of "what the…", and "yuck", and groans. Rasmus had to respond fast. He first located the motion switch for the fans and used his supernatural powers to disable it. Then he employed his spirit essence as a vacuum cleaner and did a "Hoover" job, as he had heard that the late Pittsburgh Pirate broadcaster Bob Prince formerly referred to it, sucking up as much dust as he could. He enlarged his mouth, breathed in deeply, and filled his spirit torso with the accumulated dust. He only exhaled when he raced outdoors and let it fly above and over the Allegheny River Valley below.

Of course, all the people in the sanctuary felt the suction power which filtered the air circulating about them. Unfortunately, others things went flying as well – a few scarves went up into the air, a small number of hats, and some tissue and paper items. Alex and Ian were growing more and more distraught as the service was becoming a shambles. Sadly, the worst was yet to come.

The next play that the Lady of the Church made was to attack the decorative lighting system. The Church of the Transfiguration displayed twelve lighted trees up on the chancel area. Two of these were the Christ Ornament trees, also known as *Chrismon trees*. The other ten were dressed up in solitary, but varied colors representing the green, purple, red, blue, and white Advent wreath candles. More electric candles and lighted wreaths hung in each window around the nave and along the balcony rail. What the mischievous specter decided to do was to set them blinking. Once again, the attention of the congregation was no longer focused on the worship experience. Rasmus raced around trying to find a way to correct the situation. As Ray, Cameron, and others attempted to find the cause of the disturbance, Rasmus decided that the best solution would be to just shut them all down. Pulling the plug simultaneously on each cord sent more than one question through the mystified congregation. At this point, some people were quite disturbed. Some believed that the church was experiencing a haunting. Others believed that they were the recipients of an elaborate prank. One member of the Vestry boldly ascended the chancel and angrily approached Alex and asked, "Do you know what the hell is going on here?" The member of the Vestry, of course, was correct in his reference to hell. Alex, for his part, appeared to be dumbfounded by all the disturbances. He knew, however, that the cause of these perturbations was the entity known as, "the Lady of the Church."

The sanctuary obviously was darker than before. The demon decided to act as a poltergeist and exhibit its shadowy presence throughout the sanctuary. No one was listening to Alex's Christmas Eve address as the hobgoblin cast silhouettes as she swirled around and around the sanctuary. During this phenomenon, some people left their pews and began heading for the doors. Rasmus decided that the only way to stop this was to swirl himself in the opposite direction to neutralize her effect and prohibit, at the same time, her continued movement. Crashing into each other in mid-air and comingling their distinct essences, Rasmus confronted the demon.

"Well, we meet again," Rasmus declared, speaking in a way that only the demon could hear.

"I guess it figures that you would come and try to mess up my beautiful wicked play on such a night as this," spoke the demon to Rasmus. "I should have known that it was you all along this evening."

With that, the Lady of the Church made a hasty retreat before Rasmus could say another word or speak a divine command to neutralize her actions. She simply vanished into the night. Rasmus was hopeful that her disturbances were over and that she would not attempt any more foul play during what was left of the service.

Everything was quiet as a sense of order was restored to the worshipping congregation. For his part, Alex had been praying fervently under his breath. He breathed a sigh of relief when things quieted down. At this point, all he wanted to do was to finish things up and get the congregation "the hell" out of there.

As the service worked itself around to the lighting of the Christ candle and the subsequent candle lighting ceremony, things once more went afoul. The Lady of the Church had slipped back into the building undetected by Rasmus. As the acolyte was ready to light the central Christ candle, whose light would be passed to the entire congregation, the demon breathed a column of very hot air onto this white central candle melting it into a glob of wax that oozed onto the carpeted floor. The acolyte was stunned, started backing off, and was grabbed by Hannah who came to provide assistance. Alex, who had paused the liturgy due to this circumstance, whispered instructions to Hannah. Using the blue candle, the ceremony continued as the candle-passers began the row-by-row lighting of the individual candles of the congregation. Once this was accomplished, the organist began playing the final hymn, *Silent Night*. Standing in the front row, all of a sudden Kelly's candle suddenly tipped, setting her long curly hair ablaze. As Kelly screamed, Ian grabbed the Bible on the epistle ambo, kept it open as he ran down to her, and spread it on her head. This successfully extinguished the fire in her hair, but the flames jumped from Kelly's head to his robe. Recalling the instructions when on fire to "stop, drop, and roll", Ian did just that. Only he rolled into one of the decorative trees and it immediately went up creating something similar to an intense forest fire. Ray and Cameron, among others, came running with fire extinguishers and quickly put out the blaze. However, the air in the sanctuary was now filled with smoke. Everything was also covered with the contents of the extinguishers. Truly, this was no silent night! At that, Alex shouted instructions to the congregation, bid them a Merry Christmas, and asked them to depart in peace. This would be one Christmas Eve service that no one would ever forget. But the most disturbing event of the evening was yet to occur.

As Ian was holding onto a sobbing Kelly sheltered in his arms, Brienne approached. She was immediately both confused and personally alarmed when she saw the clutching embrace of her beloved with his arms wrapped around another woman. She was instantly unsure what to make of this situation. "Ian," spoke Brienne, "let me take her into the ante-room off the sanctuary."

"No, no, I'll accompany her there," stated Ian with determination. "Please, help the others begin to clean up this place."

Ian opened the swinging door for Kelly and ushered her into the room. He attempted to sit her down, but she refused to let go of him. Then she spoke, "Thank you, Ian, for being here to save me. If you hadn't used that book to snuff out the fire on my head, I could have completely burned up! You saved my life."

"Now, let's not be too dramatic, Kelly," replied Ian. "Yes, I put out the fire with the open lectern Bible, but even if I hadn't you would not have burned up."

"You don't know that," responded Kelly. "You saved my life and now I am indebted to you. I owe you, and I am happy to be in debt to you because I love you so. There, I've said it – finally the words have passed my lips. I am in love with you, Ian. I want to be with you, and I want you to be with me. I know that you have a love connection with Brienne, but what I feel for you is very intense. I want to share in a loving relationship with you. I want you to be mine, and I want to be yours – and only yours! I am here for the taking – what do you say?"

Aghast, Ian did not know how to respond. Yes, he was very attracted to Kelly. She was very pretty and possessed a lively personality. She knew how to charm men and had a magical essence to her that he could not fully describe. She was indeed, very tempting. In fact, he could easily imagine himself being with her, but he also enjoyed a quality relationship with Brienne. He knew if he broke it off with her, she would be crushed. "Kelly, I am honored that you think so highly of me. I am also very flattered that you find me loveable. Please, I can't deal with this tonight after everything that has happened during this service. Give me some time to think about what you have shared with me. And please, do not say anything to Brienne. I do not want her to be hurt tonight or cause her any trepidation. We'll talk about this matter very soon, I promise you." Ian then gave Kelly a kiss on her forehead, broke their partial embrace, and left the room to assist the others in the clean-up job.

Walking back into the sanctuary, Alex immediately made what appeared to be both a curious and alarming request to Ian, "Ian, come up here on the chancel, I have got to show you something. Ian ascended the chancel and there on the chancel table was the church's manger scene. "Look at this, Ian," shouted Alex. "What do you see?" There before the two men was the figure of the ceramic baby Jesus in the manger melted down into a pool of liquid that had re-solidified. Alex continued to speak, "Ian, of all the strange things that have happened here tonight, this is the one thing that frightens me the most. This is the work of a demon. We have got to get rid of this thing before it destroys our ministry and the entire church." Alex was even more frightened than before. At the same time, he couldn't wait to report to Dr. Remus about the happenings on this night. "One more thing, Ian, before we join those cleaning the sanctuary," asserted Alex as he tried to divert his mind and also find something humorous in the events of the evening. "I see you take Ephesians 6:10-18 quite literally. That was very intelligent of you to use the Bible the way you did to put out the blaze on Kelly's head. As the good book says, you took up the '…shield of faith with which you can extinguish all the flaming arrows of the evil one.' The passage continues saying, 'Take the helmet of salvation and the sword of the Spirit, which is the Word of God.' I never saw the 'Word of God' used in a more dramatic way. Good thinking, Ian – you snuffed out the fires of hell!"

At that point, Brienne approached Ian. "Has Kelly settled down? Is she alright?" asked Brienne.

"Yes, she is fine," replied Ian.

"That was fast thinking, my love. You are really quick both mentally and physically," stated Brienne in admiration. Then suddenly, her mood and tone changed. "Is everything ok with us?" asked Brienne almost afraid to hear the answer. "I think that Kelly is in love with you. She hasn't said anything to me, but I can sense it. Please forgive me for probably making something out of nothing, but you know how men have disappointed me in the past. When I saw you holding her in a very dear way, well, it set off an alarm bell in my mind. You know that I have trust and confidence issues."

"Please don't worry yourself. Here, we've got a lot of clean up work to do and it's going to take some time to do it, so let's concentrate on that," declared Ian. Brienne moved to embrace Ian, but Ian turned quickly away from her as if he were trying to escape her presence and avoid any more of this uncomfortable encounter. As a result, Brienne wondered if she truly had something to worry about. For his part, Ian felt bad about not being totally honest with her, but he needed time to think before he said something that would create more difficulty for both of them.

This whole entire fire episode caught Rasmus unawares. It happened too fast for him to respond. He found himself staring at the proceedings as they quickly unfolded. He knew that her Ladyship was behind it all, but his spiritual vision was unable to locate her. He searched the edifice following the event, in what became a vain attempt to find the foul fiend. She had escaped and was nowhere to be found. All he could do now was to wait and catch Alex alone. It was obvious that they had a great deal to discuss.

As a group of men and women were cleaning and putting the church back into good order following the calamitous service, Alex noticed that Ian seemed sullen and downcast. "Ian, are you feeling alright? Is there something else bothering you besides the troubling circumstances this evening?" asked Alex.

Ian then motioned Alex to move away with him from those working to clean that area of the sanctuary. "Yes, there is Alex," replied Ian. "Tonight, Kelly expressed her love for me. I think she is a fine girl and I am really attracted to her. Don't get me wrong, I also like Brienne, and we have had a fine relationship thus far, but Kelly is the kind of woman that a man does not easily excuse and let get away. I am becoming torn between the two."

"Yes, you have a real conundrum on your hands young man," replied Alex. "Be very careful here. One of them is going to end up heartbroken, so you need to think this through rationally and in prayer. Before you say or do anything, make sure that you are settled with – and absolutely certain with - which woman you decide to choose. You know my grandfather had a very extensive vinyl record collection. One of the albums he enjoyed was from a group in the mid to late 60's known as *The Lovin' Spoonful*. One of their songs was entitled, 'Did You Ever Have to Make Up Your Mind?' The lyrics went something like this, 'Did you ever have to make up your mind? You pick up on one and leave the other behind. Its not often easy and not often kind – did you ever have to make up your mind? Did you ever have to finally decide and say yes to one and let the other one ride? There's so many changes and tears you must hide,' and on and on it goes. I liked the part when the father enters the song. It went, 'when in walks her father and takes you in line and says, better go home, son, and make up your mind.' Son, you have got to go home and make up your mind. Whatever you decide, please choose wisely and thoughtfully. And be prepared to deal as tenderly and nobly as you can with the one whose heart may be shattered by your final determination."

"Thanks, that's good advice Father McKenzie, but your words do not make the decision any easier for me," replied Ian.

"I know, this is going to be a tough one for you. I pray that God provides clarity of thought and comfort for you and the two women. Remember Ian, it is ultimately, in all probability, your decision, not God's – so do not look for any answer coming out of the blue," advised Alex. "In the meantime, let's finish our effort and get you and the others out of here. As for me, I've got some real thinking and praying to do – and all of this on this night of nights when I need to be home. Annalena is not going to be happy with me at all, but she saw what took place here tonight. I hope she realizes that I have a major problem. And I am sure that some members of the Vestry are angry with me as well. I'll have to deal with them later. It is not going to be fun – no, not at all."

The cleaning of the retardant sprayed from the fire extinguishers took more time and energy than the church members and staff first imagined. Little by little they got it cleaned up and everyone went home except for Alex. As he grabbed his papers from the pulpit he looked up at the ceiling and said out loud, "God, I certainly need your help in a big way. We could have used your help tonight, for sure! Where are you God? Where are you?" implored Alex with emphasis.

Just then Alex heard a rather loud reply. This was no gentle whisper as in Elijah's encounter with the divine. "Father McKenzie, do not fear for God has heard your supplication and has sent me to help you deal with that which troubles you." At that very moment, Father Feynman became visibly manifest before the good rector in front of the chancel area.

"Who are you? What are you?" exclaimed Alex both surprised and shocked.

"Do not be afraid, I come from above. Heaven has sent me to help you engage in spiritual warfare and rid yourselves of this demonic entity. I know this demon well. I have engaged it in two great struggles in the past. I know much about you, Father Alexander Andrew McKenzie. In this life, I was the former rector of Holy Trinity Church in Saxonburg. Allow me to introduce myself, I am the late – and now present again in this world – Father Rasmus Gilbert Feynman. I guess I am not a moment too early," expressed Rasmus.

"Wow, this night is really going to blow my mind," said a bewildered Alex as he plopped himself down on the chancel steps. Continuing, Alex exclaimed, "No, you are actually rather late. Then again, all this, and everything else that has happened to me recently is hard for me to believe and digest. And now, you show up telling me that you are from the Almighty – marvelous, simply marvelous, weird, and fantastic! My how strange my life has become!"

"I am now a saint on assignment from His Majesty providing aid and assistance where necessary. Your situation is certainly a necessary one and has garnered a great deal of attention in Heaven. Your prayers and petitions have been heard. And so, I was sent to answer them. My instructions are to work with you to take care of your nemesis – who is also my nemesis – 'the Lady of the Church,' and to do so permanently. I do mean permanently, so you have got to mind what I instruct you to say and do," stated Rasmus with emphasis.

"How long have you been here tonight, my former colleague?" asked Father McKenzie.

"I was here for the whole service," replied Rasmus. "In fact, some of the occurrences tonight I took care of for you, like re-lighting the candles…"

"Was that you?" asked Alex in a surprised manner.

"Yes, that was me," replied Rasmus. "I not only re-lit the candles down the center aisle, but I cleaned up all the dust flying around as well – after, of course, I permanently disabled the ceiling fans. Sorry about that, but you're going to have a big bill fixing them and you can't charge the expense to Heaven. I also permanently disabled the blinking lights and engaged the flying sorceress who was making all the swirling shadows around the nave. I stopped her cold on that one. Sorry about the fire. It happened too quickly for me to respond. I am happy that no one was hurt and that the damage is minimal and cosmetic. I wish I could have done more to help you at the end of the service here tonight. Unfortunately, I am sad to report that the entity escaped as well.

"I've got to ask you, Rasmus, what is a saint doing in the service of Heaven back here on Earth? I thought that this was only in the 'modus operandi' of angels. And exactly what are you now – a ghost? And if you are a ghost, you'd better explain to me your peculiar usage by Heaven. I did not think that once deceased, human beings could return as ghosts to this planet for any reason at all," said Father McKenzie. "I thought that once you passed over, that was it – period."

"You know the Scriptures," started Feynman. "We have after death appearances by Samuel, Moses, and Elijah. When God wants you to serve on a specific mission in a specific locale, God will not be denied."

"Some commentators conclude that Samuel's appearance, as recorded in First Samuel 28:7-25, before the conjuring Witch of Endor, was not actually Samuel at all," asserted Alex.

"Please look at the text carefully, Father McKenzie. The ghost was indeed that of Samuel," expressed Feynman rather matter-of-factly. "No one was more surprised at his appearance than the witch."

"Yes, I am the answer to your prayer, and I am going to do for you what Von Steuben did for George Washington at Valley Forge," asserted Rasmus.

"What was that?" asked McKenzie with a puzzled look on his face.

"At Valley Forge, Washington was a man of intense prayer. He was seen numerous times by the local farmers kneeling and walking with his horse, petitioning Providence. The General needed a great deal of help. He came to rely on Heaven's assistance. Von Steuben was a significant part of Washington's prayer answer. Now, Von Steuben was not exactly a godly man and he had a long list of sins. Yet God used this very imperfect man to do what no one else could do for Washington's Continental Army. Von Steuben made them an army. He made them into an efficient fighting force that could wage battle correctly and maneuver in an expert manner. While most historians do not recognize it, in the aftermath of the Battle of Monmouth in New Jersey, the forces at George Washington's command had become the best army in the world due in large part to Von Steuben. The British General Clinton certainly realized it and was afraid to stand up against Washington in an open field pitched battle on the American coastal plain. In fact, he never did challenge Washington again. Von Steuben brought a great deal of know how to the table. Yet, so often, it is not only what you bring to the table that counts. It's what you do with what you have, and what you learn that you can add to the table during your life that matters. That is one of the reasons I am here for you. I am going to add to your library of knowledge. We are going to help each other to beat this monster, cast it out from our midst, and put it away permanently. My grandfather was a big Johnny Weissmuller fan. Do you know who Johnny Weissmuller was?" asked Rasmus.

"No, I do not," answered McKenzie.

"He was an undefeated American Olympian who won five gold medals in swimming and more than 60 world titles in addition to more than 50 national titles. My grandfather and I thought he was the best of the old-time characters who played Tarzan in those old 1930's and 1940's black and white movies. He certainly came up with the best Tarzan yell. That's the one Carol Burnett was able to imitate fairly accurately. I hope you know who Carol Burnett is?" Alex nodded assent. "One of my best quotes from the so-called 'ape man' was when he was confronted with a group of Nazi soldiers in the 1943 movie, 'Tarzan Triumphs'. In this movie Tarzan states, after being shot at and his son taken prisoner, the once famous line, 'Now Tarzan make war.' That is exactly what you are going to do, Father McKenzie. I am going to make sure that you know how to make war against this fiend, and you are going to help me imprison it!"

Rasmus then explained at some length the finer points of spiritual warfare. He made sure that Father McKenzie was as comfortable as possible with everything he shared with him and the plan moving forward. Rasmus had no problem with someone who had the caliber of Dr. Remus to be present and help lead the expulsion and capture of the monster. Alex asked Feynman if he thought that Jillian Jiganie should be invited to attend and help because she had so effectively handled the entity a few days beforehand. Alex explained that Father Fairlamb wanted nothing to do with the entity and refused to help in any direct way. Rasmus affirmed that it was fine with him if Jillian were invited and decided to attend the proceedings. He left it up entirely, however, to Father McKenzie. Finally, as it was now past midnight, Rasmus said to Alex, "You better take your leave and get home to Annalena. I'll spend Christmas Day right here in the Church blessing it, guarding it, and being on the lookout for our Lady if she happens to return to this haunt. Have a Merry Christmas and I'll be with you on the 26th." With that, Alex bid Feynman a good night. As he did so, he pondered quietly just how one does bid a ghost a good night.

When Alex returned home, Annalena was very involved in the Christmas Day preparations for their children and guests. Annalena was disturbed at his lateness, but under the circumstances, decided not to make an issue of it. She had witnessed the service and felt both bad and frightened at the thought of what happened.

"Is everything fine at the church, honey?" she asked as Alex came through the door.

"I am sorry that I am so late, dear, but I don't know how to express to you what just happened to me," Alex replied.

"Don't tell me that Katrina showed up after the service with another problem," alleged Annalena.

"No, no – I did have another visitor, but it wasn't Katrina or Hugh or any other person," announced Alex.

"If it wasn't any other person – then who or what came to visit?" a wide-eyed Annalena inquired.

"You know very well how intensely I have been praying to Heaven for help to deliver us from this entity that has come our way. Well, Heaven sent me an answer. No, I didn't have an encounter with Almighty God, hear a voice, or see some anthropomorphism. You are, however, not going to believe this. I have trouble believing this myself, but I just lived it for the past hour or so. Are you ready for this? Heaven sent me a ghost. The answer to my prayer has come via a heaven-sent ghostly being. He was formerly, in this life, that deceased priest from Saxonburg who fell to his death a few years ago. At least he claims he is the spirit of that priest – one Rasmus Feynman. He is a very friendly ghost, I must say. I have never met a ghost before. He is here to help us with our demonic haunting. He talked to me at length about spiritual warfare and the deliverance ministry. On the day after Christmas, we will try to extricate ourselves from this dilemma. Now, let me help you finish the preparations for Christmas day and let's get to bed. Hopefully I can get some sleep – I am pretty keyed up right now. I am sorry I have not been more of a help to you this night," said Alex apologetically.

"That's ok, Alex, I understand that things went very badly tonight and that you have some very deep concerns. I happen to be very fearful myself, my dear. I am afraid for us, our family, and for you. The circumstances at the church really shook me up tonight. I don't know how well I will sleep either, but I will be happy to have you right by my side," expressed Annalena with love.

The couple finished their preparations while Annalena plied him with many questions about the ghost, so great was her curiosity. When they finished, they gathered themselves for bed to at least get a few moments of rest. It had been a fitful night for both of them. Annalena eventually got off to sleep and enjoyed some much-needed rest, even if it was very brief. Alex, however, failed to secure a much needed "long winter's nap."

Stave 10

Now Tarzan
Make War

hristmas Day was a busy one for Alex and Annalena, their children, and their extended family. Alex was quite tired all day long from having a very late night. Once he returned home on Christmas Eve, he had a great deal to do to prepare Christmas morning for the children. He took so long in making preparations and putting toys together in order to make a grand presentation that Annalena was concerned that he might not make it into bed before the children arose. Alex made it to bed just before the morning sun appeared over the horizon, but was too hyper to fall asleep. The next thing he knew, the children were awake. Christmas Day was not as much fun for Alex as he had imagined it would be just a few days earlier. The prospect of having to use the phone on Christmas Day in order to make arrangements for a second attempt to eliminate the demonic entity attached to Katrina was not a happy thought. In fact, the entire deliverance procedure hung over his head so much that he could barely enjoy the day with his family. He made his best attempt to refrain from being cranky, and feigned much enjoyment as he and Annalena hosted the day's events. By the time evening came and his wife and children were basking in the glow of Christmas night, he could barely stay awake and soon was out like a light.

Alex was eventually able to contact everyone on Christmas Day in order to set a time to meet on the 26th. This included Jillian Jiganie. However, she declined to attend. Her fiancé was dead set against her involvement in the deliverance exercise, though Jillian would have agreed to attend had Jeff not been so adamant about her non-participation. Alex wanted as many people to be present who had any great spiritual connection going for them with God. After the circumstances on Christmas Eve, Alex thought it advisable to invite Ian to join with himself, Dr. Remus, and the Helmans to help release Katrina and expel any and all demonic entities that had attached themselves to her.

The next thing that Alex knew, it was the morning of the 26th. Originally, this was a day he had planned to take off, but everyone agreed to meet at the church at 10 a.m. to get this thing finished. Alex arrived at the church at 7 a.m. to prepare himself for the ordeal. He reminded himself that it was St. Stephen's Day. He pondered about the first martyr of the church for a minute or two, recalling the good saint's fight with the Jewish ruling body, the Sanhedrin. He had his own fight this day, and he hoped it did not end with himself, or any of the others, becoming casualties of the spiritual warfare they were about to engage. It was also "Boxing Day". He realized that early in the afternoon, several ladies, as well as Ray and Cameron, would be present in the church to deliver the collected offering of material and financial resources to the local Habitat for Humanity ministry in Parnassus, the Allegheny Valley Association of Churches Food Bank in Natrona Heights and the Hope Center in Tarentum. Alex hoped and prayed that their work of deliverance would be concluded prior to the arrival of these Boxing Day volunteers.

Some time prior to 10 a.m., Alex heard a knock at his office door. He called out from his seated position at his desk, "Who is there?"

"It's just me, your new colleague, Rasmus," Feynman responded.

"Come on in," Alex answered.

Opening the door, a fully materialized Rasmus walked into the room and before he sat down in a chair in front of Father McKenzie's desk, the two of them shook hands. It was a greeting that Alex thought was a very strange and curious phenomenon under the circumstances. Shaking hands with a ghost in some form of corporeal manifestation had to be undeniably rare. Alex had now experienced the ghost in three forms: invisible; translucent; and at present, physical.

"Are you ready for today's engagement?" Rasmus asked Father McKenzie. "Remember what I have shared with you. Remember what you must do. It is critical that you do it!"

"Yes, thank you, I think I am prepared," responded Alex. "Also, I will not forget what the final outcome of this encounter is to be!"

"I want to assure you that I will be with you in the room; although I will be invisible, of course," stated Rasmus.

"Yes, of course," replied Alex.

"I do not plan to reveal myself to any of the others, but I will be communicating with you, if needed, as the situation progresses," said Rasmus. "Be well assured that if it becomes necessary, I will help guide you. Please take confidence in my presence."

"I am certainly happy to have it," responded Alex with a smile breaking out on his face.

"I'll just quietly fade away right now as the rest of the company is about to enter," stated Rasmus. As he finished his words, he began to take on invisibility once more.

Everyone arrived as the hour reached the time agreed upon. Once again, everyone was very nervous. Katrina, however, seemed to be quite upset. She explained to Dr. Remus, Alex, and Ian that her daughter Moriah had commented about an invisible friend named "Piggie", who was visiting with her in her bedroom. Moriah seemed very enchanted with her new friend. Piggie told Moriah that her mother wanted to send her away and she hoped her mother's actions would not disturb their new friendship and playtime together. Moriah then begged her parents not to chase Piggie out of their house. Obviously, Hugh and Katrina were very upset about what seemed to them to be a new demonic incursion upon their family. "I don't get this pig thing," stated Katrina.

"It reminds me of the story of the Gerasenes demoniac – you know where the demons entered the pigs. Let me check in my Bible," stated Alex as he began to fumble through his Bible notes. "Yes, the story appears in all three of the Synoptics – Matthew 8:28-34, Mark 5:1-20, and Luke 8:26-39."

"It is interesting that you have made reference to this story, Alex," stated Dr. Remus. "The pigs represent what is unclean in Jewish culture and what may be unclean in terms of the demons in the story. However, It is the demons who beg to go into the pigs as Jesus acquiesces to their request."

"I have always found that is most odd," stated Ian.

"Yes," responded Dr. Remus. "There is so much going on in this story. Allow me to explain some of it to you. It appears that since God took on human flesh in the person of Jesus, there had been an increase in demonic activity as these foul entities desired to imitate the incarnation. Their whole purpose seems to be to oppose the work of Jesus. Their objective is to destroy. Demons feed on destruction. In our case, they want to destroy people like yourself, Katrina. They want to destroy your family, Hugh. They want to destroy your family as well, Alex. They also want to destroy this ministry and this church. The arrival of Jesus to that location in the Gospel stories changed everything. In the Matthean account, there are two men who are possessed. Only one man is mentioned in the other two accounts. Mark and Luke concentrate their stories solely on him. Maybe it is because the man wants to travel with Jesus after his deliverance. We really do not know. It reminds me somewhat of the two criminals crucified alongside Jesus. One of them chastises Jesus, while the other one acknowledges his Lordship and begs for divine mercy. One of the men is redeemed. The other is not, and he is largely forgotten."

"At first, it appears that only one demon is in play, and then we find out that there are many," interjected Alex.

"Yes," continued Dr. Remus, "the demons knew exactly who Jesus was – God in human flesh. They knew who was boss. They were also aware of their pending doom due to their alliance with Lucifer and their rebellion against God. Therefore, they try to avoid confinement in the Abyss as long as possible. This is mentioned in Luke 8:31, Revelation 9:1-6 and 20:1-3. The Abyss, of course, is another name for Hell and the Place of Judgment. It is synonymous with the Lake of Fire in Revelation 20:10 and 21:8. The demons were powerless and terror-stricken in the presence of Jesus. They who had terrorized and so ill-treated this poor man now beg Jesus for mercy. And so, Jesus demands to know their name."

"What is so important about knowing their name?" interrupted Ian. "And is Jesus asking the man for his name, or is he asking for the name of the demon to be revealed?"

Dr. Remus continued, "Perhaps if Jesus is asking the man for his name, Jesus is communicating to him that he has an identity apart from the demons. However, it is the demons who answer. One's name is sacred in many cultures. To know the name can also be an attempt to gain control over the person and his or her soul. Knowing a name can give someone, or some entity, a little bit of a hold on you and some power over you. As a result, they have partial possession of something that belongs to you that was originally yours alone. On the other hand, if Jesus is demanding to know the name or names of the demons, he is letting them know that he is in charge. This demonstration in verbalizing the name or names may also be for the townsfolk who were observing and listening intently to this encounter. Maybe Jesus was trying to share with them the real circumstances concerning this man. Because Jesus already knew exactly who they were and what they were up to, the demons couldn't obfuscate or lie to him. Of course, Jesus did not need to know the names of the demonic entities to cast them out and put them away. Once again, with so many other people around who were witnessing this encounter, Jesus wanted everyone present to be as clear as possible as to what was truly going on. Satan is secretive, slippery, and sinuous. He specializes in hiding in the shadows. Jesus, on the other hand, operates in the light and is completely revelatory and open."

"And so, like we discovered the last time we met, the man was possessed by many demons," offered Alex. "A Roman Legion, depending on the particular period of time in history and also based on military necessity, could be anywhere from a couple thousand men up to 11,000 soldiers, counting all their auxiliary troops. Normally, it was somewhere around 4,500 and 6,000 men if you count support troops and calvary."

"You are correct, my friend," responded Dr. Remus. James then continued, "The severity of the possessed man's affliction appears to be in proportion with the number of demons that have attached themselves to him. These demons know they are powerless before the incarnate God. Perhaps by employing the term 'Legion', they might be making an appeal to Jesus to be compassionate. Perhaps they may be using the terms evasively in an attempt to withhold their true identity and re-direct his attention. What these demonic entities would like to do is thwart his power to pronounce judgment on them."

"What about the pigs?" asks Katrina.

"Well," continued James "they beg Jesus not to be sent to the Abyss. You see, these adherents to the evil empire are unable to do anything without Christ's permission."

At this, Feynman, who was at the left ear of Alex, whispered, "The enemy of our souls is under the complete control of God and can only act in the ways that God allows. I hope this gives you extra confidence, my good man."

Alex then nodded affirmatively, as if to no one in particular.

"Do not blame Jesus for killing the swine," continued James. "I think Jesus permitted this to show all the witnesses – the townsfolk, the herders, his disciples and followers, and the man himself the destructive power that was inside the possessed individual, and that he was now finally clear and clean. The demons' destructive work did continue, but not upon the man. The pigs, it would appear without any power to resist and fight back, go crazy immediately after the demons attach themselves to them. They run off a ledge and into the lake killing themselves. They were easy prey because they could not offer any resistance to the entities at all. We must also note here that the demons could not control the pigs either. Their end is their own destruction. We might be able to conclude here that without any bodies to possess, they ended up going to where they begged not to go; although the text does not indicate what happened to these entities after the death of the pigs. What I think the *text* does indicate is that without God, we humans can also rush headlong toward our own destruction. We must note, however, that there is an alternative view to what I have just revealed to you. In reality, pigs are highly intelligent creatures and they can swim. What if the destruction of the pigs was one of sacrifice on their part? Pigs were used by the Gentiles, particularly the Romans, for food, and slaughtered in pagan religious ceremonies. What if the death of the pigs is, in reality, a self-sacrifice on their part which prefigures the self-sacrifice of Jesus on the cross? What if the destruction of the legion of demons pre-figures the destruction of the Greco/Roman sacrificial and religious system which was very much Satanic in origin and practice? The pigs in this story may actually be rather heroic instead of victims. I don't know. I offer this up to you because there is a great deal more here to think about than one might imagine!" With that, James finished his analysis of these texts for those in the room.

Unbeknownst to all, Feynman bore a big smile on his face knowing that Dr. James Remus had fairly and accurately explained the text, including the various opinions of many biblical commentators.

Turning toward Katrina, Dr. Remus stated, "I know I have not completely answered your question in terms of the connection between the demonic and their employment of pigs as a symbol, but enough of this – we aren't here for me to continue this Bible study lesson."

"I completely agree, Dr. Remus. Let's get down to business right now, shall we? I want to get these foul creatures detached from me and my family," cried Katrina.

"We need to first start with prayer," stated Dr. Remus. He then led the group in a long and powerful prayer taking command over the environment and the situation. He also bound the demonic to that particular room lest an escape attempt was hurriedly implemented by any or all of the foul entities. Alex also added some words to the prayer as Rasmus whispered some additional thoughts in his ear.

It was at this point that the real engagement began. Thus far, Katrina had been in her own mind and in full possession of her faculties.

As Dr. Remus began, he stated to those present, "Remember, in Jesus Christ we must be respectful of the authority we possess and humble in knowing that we do not have any divine power in and of ourselves to defeat the spiritual enemies of the Christ. Jesus does, and Jesus does alone! Also, remember that our Christ is God. For a long time in this world, our predecessors concentrated too much on the divinity of Jesus. They failed to pay attention to his humanity. Today, the problem is reverse – there is too much concentration on his humanity to the sacrifice of his divinity. On this very day, we must call upon and experience Jesus' attributes as the almighty God. Therefore, through the Holy Spirit, in the name of Jesus, and by the presence of the Father, no demonic force can stand against us. When arrayed against the Trinity, no other power stands a chance. When we are totally immersed in the Triune God, as God's stewards and servants on mission by our heavenly Sovereign, no demonic force can defeat us. Remember all these things and let us proceed with confidence, shall we?"

Dr. Remus then looked at Katrina and began to speak to the demons that were haunting her. As he did so, a very strange phenomenon began to occur. At times, it seemed like the entities were taking control of Katrina with her involuntary, sudden and strange head movements, as well as the alien voice that proceeded from her mouth. The names of each demon began to be given up one by one. They were certainly strange names and often offensive to both the ear and sensibility. At other times, Katrina, in her right mind, would offer up names of those entities she had come to learn were attached to her. This went on for some time. At no time, did the demon known as "Leviathan", otherwise named as "the Lady of the Church", make an appearance.

Finally, Rasmus became alarmed at what was taking place. He quietly directed and pointed out to Father McKenzie that the minions of the central demonic figure were offering up the lower entities to tire the deliverance ministry team to redirect them from the main offender they were after. The minions were also trying to employ delay tactics to get the team to think that they had emptied the well and had removed them all. Alex whispered this to Dr. Remus, who responded by saying, "You are correct in your assessment, my good man!"

Time was also moving along. It was now early afternoon, and soon a group of women and men would be in the church to pack up the Boxing Day material and donations. This occurrence could disturb the whole proceeding. The Lady of the Church also knew that the presence of other people in the building could short-circuit their removal effort. All she had to do was drag things out until these people came around to provide interruption and a pretext for the closure of this exercise. She reasoned that this might cause the extraction group to cease and desist due to both privacy concerns and not to raise alarm.

Feynman whispered to Alex, "Push him Alex – push Dr. Remus into taking greater action. He must go after this entity with passion and zeal and not hesitate to remove it. He must push on boldly. If he doesn't, you need to take over and press the issue! Remember Tarzan – it is time for you to make war!"

Rasmus was standing behind Father McKenzie, who was seated. No one else knew that the late Father Feynman was in the room except for the Lady of the Church. As Dr. Remus began to ramp up his assault on the remaining entities, Alex joined the fray, commanding the extraction of the Leviathan. He knew that if this demon was extracted, the other remaining entities would probably depart as well, or they would be much easier to remove by the deliverance team. It was if the two men, James and Alex, were double-teaming the primary demonic entity. It was at this point that the Lady of the Church took full possession of Katrina's faculties and sinisterly spoke to Feynman trying to buy time as people began entering the church. "I see that you are also here – you pathetic little weasel," said the demon. Katrina's body-controlled focus seemed to be speaking at the empty space above where Alex was seated.

"Who is it talking to?" cried Ian.

"I don't know," exclaimed Hugh.

"Is there some other entity we have not recognized in this room with us?" asked Ian suggestively.

"If so, I hope it is an angel of the Lord," replied Hugh.

Feynman then spoke to the Lady of the Church directly, but outside of the ability of those in the room to hear what he was saying. "This time you are not going to make an escape. We are going to send you to where you belong! The time of your imprisonment, awaiting judgment, has arrived!"

At Feynman's pronouncement, the Lady of the Church, using Katrina's faculties, let out a blood-curdling cry and scream. It was very loud, reverberating all through the church. All of those who had entered the church heard it and stopped what they were doing. Ray, Cameron, Kelly, Hannah, Brienne, and the others, gathered as a group with a puzzled expression on their faces. Ray volunteered to go to the closed library door and knocked. Immediately Alex shouted, "Please do not disturb us, we are conducting important business here. Everything is alright. Go back to what you are doing and we will tell you what we can about this later."

"Ok," remarked Ray, through the shuttered door. "There are several of us here, if you need help! Just let us know!"

"Thank you, but that will not be necessary," replied Alex.

The Lady of the Church caused Katrina's body to thrash about in the chair. Releasing some terrifying screams, Katrina crashed onto the floor.

Hugh and Ian gathered on either side of her and tried to hold her still. With her left arm the demon- oppressed figure launched Hugh through the air, crashing into the book shelves. With her right arm, Katrina's overpowered body sent Ian hurtling toward the door. He slammed up against it, hitting it with great force. Katrina then stood up, displaying a ferocious look on her face focused in the direction of Alex and Rasmus. She began to slowly levitate in a vertical position, rising upward toward the ceiling.

Just at this moment, responding to the loud bang the group of willing workers heard on the library door, Kelly, who had always been very gregarious, inquisitive, and bold, decided to investigate what was going on in that room. She attempted to open the door, crashing into Ian on the other side. Ian rolled out of the way while trying to stand up. With his movement unblocking the passageway, Kelly fully opened the door and entered the room. Aghast at what she saw, she stopped dead in her tracks and covered her mouth with her hands as she inhaled and held her breath. From her levitating position the demon immediately jerked her head toward the doorway and resolutely stared at Kelly. She pointed her finger at Kelly, which sent her flying out of the room and hitting the wall beyond. Immediately after crashing into the wall, Kelly slumped down onto the floor and was obviously hurt.

Ian, still not on his feet, scampered out of the room on all fours and reached out to grab Kelly's limp body. He wrapped his arms around the stunned and injured female, trying to nurse her back into full consciousness.

At this, Alex knew he had to act fast. Standing up and pointing at Katrina, he pronounced the words that bind the spirit with the power of the Christ. Having taken authority in the name of Jesus over the entity, he referenced the sacrifice of Jesus on the cross which produced the ultimate victory of God over Satan. Then he said, "In the name of Jesus, my Savior and Lord, I command all of you to come out of her. I command all of you in the name of Jesus to go immediately into the Abyss." Referencing the Lady of the Church, Alex continued, "You and your minions are never to return. This I command in the name and through the power of Jesus Christ! I also speak against and break this terrible curse placed upon us by Boara the witch, in the name of Jesus. In the name of Jesus, I send this curse also into the pit of hell. This curse is now and forever broken. It shall plague us no more! I plead this in the precious name of Jesus the Christ, the Son of our militant shepherd Father God, who alone is our redeemer and sustainer.

The entity let out one more hellacious yell and cried out, "No, no, no." Instantaneously, silence ruled as Katrina's body fell out of the air and collapsed on the floor. Alex was close enough, and quick enough, to break Katrina's fall. Placing her down on the floor while supporting her neck and limp head, Katrina woke up having taken, once again, full possession of her faculties. "What happened? Why am I lying here on the floor?"

"It's over, my friend. The demons are gone. The powers of Heaven have removed them. You are free," stated Alex with tears in his eyes. "God has done a marvelous work here. God has liberated you, and your family, and has taken away the generations-long curse."

Alex looked in the direction of Rasmus. Only he could see Rasmus' spiritual countenance. Rasmus was smiling and nodding his head in agreement.

Katrina knew nothing about what had happened to Hugh. He was bleeding slightly from his head and face due to some of the books and decorative objects on the shelves falling on and cutting him. Katrina also knew nothing about what had happened to Ian. He had a lump on the back of his head, but otherwise seemed to be no worse for wear as he cared for Kelly. Picking Katrina up and helping her to a chair, the three men who remained in the room congratulated each other. Dr. Remus thanked Alex for his sudden surge in spiritual energy, putting an end to the confrontation. The three men then laid their hands on Katrina as they gathered around her and offered up a prayer of healing and thanksgiving to God. It was quite a praise-filled expression of joy, and one of sheer delight in the God of their salvation. This was a moment in time that none of them would ever forget. It would be deeply inscribed upon their memory. Indeed, it would be a high point in their spiritual life and experience, revealing to them the true presence and power of their God of grace, mercy, forgiveness, and love – a God who would not only fight for them, but fight with them as well.

Rasmus joined them in prayer and in celebration. Of course, Alex knew that Rasmus was there with them. Rasmus, for his part, was delighted that he had finally accomplished his full mission. Before he returned to the intermediate heaven, he wanted to have another private conversation with Alex, but that would have to wait until he could get Alex alone again.

The attention of the small group immediately centered around Ian and Kelly. Ian was sitting on the floor with Kelly's head on his lap. Ray, Cameron, Hannah, and Brienne also arrived at the location, staring down at the two of them on the floor.

"What in the world is going on here?" asked Ray.

"I'll explain it all to you later, Ray," responded Alex. "You are in for quite a story!"

Brienne was concerned about Kelly, but she wondered to herself if Kelly was milking the situation for all she could get lying there in the arms of Ian. Disgusted, she walked off, privately fearing that this might be the beginning of the end of her love connection with Ian.

Hannah then returned to the scene with a wet compress for Kelly's head. "Is she going to be alright?" Hannah asked Ian.

Before Ian could answer, Kelly replied, "I think I am going to be fine. Please just give me some time to compose myself, stop shaking as you can see, and settle myself down."

Kelly looked up at Ian, who was looking down and smiling at her. "You've got to explain to me what just happened here."

"I will – right now just take a moment or two to recover yourself," responded Ian.

"Thank you for coming to my aid," said Kelly. "You know that I love you so very much. I hope that you now love me too. I feel so comfortable in your arms. I'd like to stay like this forever. Please tell me that you love me. I know that Brienne is a very fine person, but I think we can be a better match for each other. What do you think?"

"Kelly, you are a fine girl," Ian tenderly stated. "I cannot deny that I am attracted to you – both in terms of your person and your marvelous appearance, but I have thought long and hard about this over the past couple of days, and I have decided to stay with Brienne. I think that you and I would make a fine couple and that we would do well together, but my heart is with her. She is the one whom I love. Please understand, this is not a rejection of you. You are a wonderful lady and any man would be most fortunate to be in a relationship with you. My heart belongs to Brienne. I can't and won't disappoint her and break her heart. She really does mean a lot to me. In fact, I think it is time I ask her to marry me."

With a tear rolling down her cheek, Kelly responded, "I understand, Ian. I will always have a love for you in my heart. Please do not blame me for trying. It is out of my great affection for you and nothing else. I think it is time you shared with Brienne what you just shared with me. I wish you both all the happiness in the world. I guess we better get up and join the others now. Thank you for coming to my rescue."

The two helped each other up and joined the rest of the group engaged in great conversation. Ray and Cameron were passing around coffee for everyone as Hannah was helping Katrina treat Hugh's wounds in the restroom. Ian moved to Brienne's side, and placed his right arm around her waist and smiled at her. With Ian's action and behavior, Brienne drew some renewed confidence in their continuing relationship. Alex gave the group of volunteers a "cliff notes" type summary version of what had transpired. He asked them not to retell the story and to refrain from spreading any gossip about the event. It was now obvious to all that Katrina was the main focus of interest here. This could no longer be hidden from those who partially witnessed the proceedings.

Alex did what he could to keep much of what happened to Katrina as private as possible.

Soon, it was back to work for the willing volunteers. They had to finish packing the materials and delivering the goods and the money around the valley.

Dr. James Remus shook hands with Alex and said to him before he left, "You know Alex, I could use someone with your determination and skill to be by my side in this ministry. Do you have any interest in joining my team and working with me?"

Laughing, Alex responded, "No – sorry, I do not – this was enough for me. However, be assured that I will not hesitate to call upon you if I run into anything like this circumstance again. Thank you for all of your help, advice, time, and effort. You are truly one of God's special warriors and an amazing individual! Have a terrific remainder of the Christmas season!"

Alex gathered with Katrina as he and Hugh shared with her all the events of the day about which she knew little. Katrina was most appreciative of the support, help, and deliverance she received. The Helmans left Alex's office, smiling. They were glad that it was all over. On their way home, Katrina and Hugh decided to buy Moriah a big stuffed animal as a new playmate. They both agreed that the stuffed animal they purchased would not be that of a pig!

After some time went by, Alex was finally alone in his office. Once more taking on material form, Rasmus knocked on the door, which was slightly ajar. "May I enter, Alex?" asked Rasmus, poking his head through the threshold. .

"Sure, come in and have a seat. Wow, that was something, wasn't it, my good saint?" asked Alex rhetorically. "Boy, am I glad that it's over!"

"You were fantastic, Alex. You were absolutely fantastic!" exclaimed Rasmus with glee. "Now I can go back to the intermediate heaven and present to my superiors a full and final report. We accomplished everything we had set out to perform, my good man!"

"How soon do you have to depart, Rasmus?" questioned Alex.

"I must leave you very soon, but before I go, I would like to pray with you in order to bless your ministry and this church. I also have a particular request that I hope you will agree to accomplish for me. Could I borrow a piece of paper and a pen?" asked Rasmus.

"Sure, right here," responded Alex, as he pushed some stationery and a pen on his desk toward Rasmus.

Taking pen and paper in hand, Rasmus wrote down several lines and handed his composition to Alex. "Here, please personally take this missive to the person and address I have written on this piece of paper," stated Rasmus.

"I sure will," said Alex. "Will I ever see you again, Rasmus?"

"On this side of life, it is most doubtful, but one never knows what predicaments you might get into in the future, and what assignments I might be given in response," stated Feynman with a giant smile on his face. "I will certainly see you at the ingathering of the saints. You can rest assured of that! It is time for me to depart. Let me pray right this moment for you, your family, your ministry, and your church. And please, take good care of that wife of yours. She is very special and needs the 'double A's'."

"The 'double A's' - what are the 'double A's'?" Alex asked with a puzzled look on his face.

"Attention and affection my good man. Every wife needs attention and affection. Make sure you present her with a great deal of both!" asserted Rasmus.

"Yes," agreed Alex, "I certainly will!"

Following a time of prayer and blessing, Feynman bid Alex farewell and quickly dematerialized.

Alex found himself missing the dear saint immediately, but he knew that in God's good time they would be together again. As it is at the end of the eighth chapter of Romans, Paul records his view that in Jesus Christ there is "no separation". The good news is that the Trinity, the Heavenly host, and all of God's saints will enjoy a renewed life together the way God intended it to be in the first place; this time, forever!

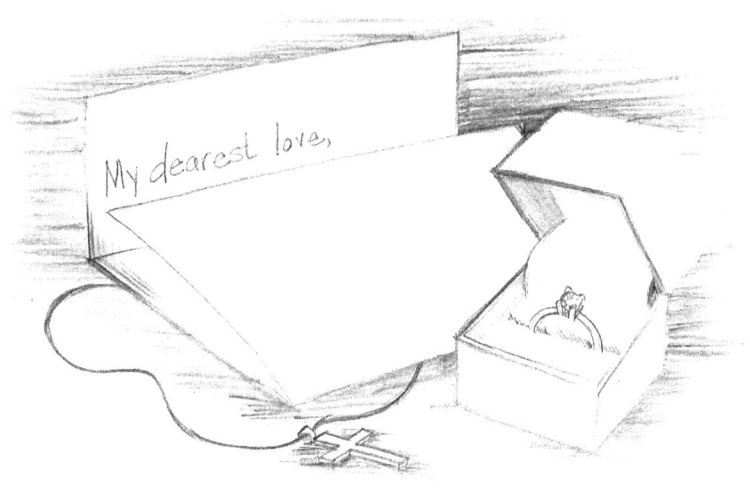

Stave 11

The Conclusion
of the Matter

Finally, Alex could relax. After cleaning up the things that fell and broke in the library, Alex went home, intent on practicing the "double A's" with his wife and children. Though he was exhausted, he found he could now actually enjoy this season of hope renewed and peace secured.

The very next day, Alex purchased four silver cross necklaces for the ladies involved in the drama. To celebrate their victory, he purchased a cross necklace for Annalena, one for Katrina, and ones for both Kendall and Moriah to wear in the future. All four crosses were prayed over and blessed as Alex asked the Lord to keep these ladies free from the Evil One. He did the same for his sons, purchasing two suit collar cross pins for them to wear in the coming years. He also prayed that his two boys would be dedicated to the Lord and valiant in the face of evil.

Alex was a very creative romantic. Throughout his marriage to Annalena, he had dreamed up many ways to gift his wife for the purpose of communicating his love for her. He believed that love needed to be expressed in terms of action and not solely based upon the spoken word. Telling his wife that he loved her was part of Alex's everyday practice. Expressing love in creative action and through service was something he believed to be vital as well. At this moment in their marriage, he also felt that his wife needed some loving attention based on everything that had transpired recently. "Putting love into practice in some creative way is what lovers are supposed to do," he reasoned to himself. Since they were now moving through the Twelve Days of Christmas, Alex came up with a unique gift idea. Anglicans were never known to be enthusiastic participants in the Temperance Movement in America during the 19th and 20th centuries. Anglicans were not known for being teetotalers. Annalena enjoyed a good glass of wine in the evening on occasion. Alex decided to purchase 12 bottles of wine and hide them around the house. Mimicking the work of legendary characters such as Santa Claus, the Easter Bunny, and the Tooth Fairy, he created the creature known as the "Wine Weasel". The Wine

Weasel was a magical animal who gifted worthy women with a bottle of wine and hid his gift offerings in the houses of his recipients. During the twelve-day season, every time Annalena discovered a bottle of wine in their residence, Alex exclaimed, "It must be the work of the Wine Weasel." Thus, a new tradition was born in the McKenzie household – a tradition that further endeared Annalena to her husband.

Ian, during the same time, quickly made and secured a reservation for dinner at the Bloser Mansion in New Kensington. He made a hasty visit to Seita Jewelers in Tarentum where he purchased a big surprise for Brienne. The two of them shared a very emotionally-charged dinner together. Ian had communicated with Brienne that the two of them had to talk. He indicated that they would do so during dinner at this restaurant which also served as a bed and breakfast. Brienne, with her past history of disappointment in men always front and center on her mind, thought that Ian might be explaining to her the parting of their ways that evening. Anxiety-ridden, she was very much on edge that night. After they had ordered their meals and drinks, Brienne pushed the conversation forward. "Ian, I know that you invited me here to share something important with me. If you are planning on breaking up with me, please just tell me and don't play around with my emotions. Right now, I am just sick with worry!"

"Break up with you – break up with you," repeated a surprised Ian with astonishment all over his face. "I didn't bring you here to break if off with you. I brought you here to ask you if you would agree in making our relationship stronger and more permanent – much more permanent, in fact! I love you Brienne, and I want to marry you."

As Ian said these words, he left his seat and bowed down on one knee. From his suit jacket pocket, he produced a small box and opened it up facing Brienne. Placing her hands on her face in awe, she began to cry as she looked at the diamond engagement ring.

"Brienne, I am crazy in love with you – and only you. Will you do me the honor of marrying me?" asked Ian, now also with tears in his eyes.

"Yes, yes, yes," shouted Brienne as she rose out of her chair and grabbed Ian who was also rising from his kneeling position. "I would be honored to be your wife. Yes, I will marry you. I am so surprised, I thought you might be breaking up with me. I thought you might be ending it with me so you could be with Kelly."

"No, not at all," replied Ian. "Kelly is a fine girl, and what a good wife she would be for someone else, but not me. In fact, I have someone in mind for Kelly."

"Who is he?" asked Brienne.

"You know him – my good friend, Donald," exclaimed Ian. "I think that the two of them would complement each other very well! I plan to introduce them to each other very soon. Perhaps you can help me with that?"

"Oh, would I," responded Brienne quickly and emphatically, breathing a sigh of relief.

Ian and Brienne did introduce Kelly to a man named Donald Lockhart one week later. He was, in fact, a distant relative of the late actress with the same last name. The two ended up making an interesting couple. If it is true that opposites attract, then this couple were perfect for each other.

Hannah continued to participate in the church and met her future husband, David, there. While she worked in finance and banking as a career choice, she became very interested in pursuing Christian Education as an avocation. Alex, of course, was the officiant of their wedding.

Hugh and Katrina were no longer plagued by demons and spirits, though it became obvious to them that their daughter Moriah seemed to be quite sensitive to the spiritual world. In turn, they kept a keen eye on her, maintained her attendance at the church, and taught her much from the Bible. She grew up to be a delightful person and a great adherent to the faith. Katrina and Alex continued their friendship. The good news is that their friendship was no longer viewed as a threat by Annalena.

Annalena and Alex continued their upbringing of Kendall, Theodore, and Truman. Alex practiced the "double A's" with his wife and children. He did so with much more personal intent and vigor, making life much happier for all.

Ray and Cameron continued their work with the youth groups and other aspects of ministry within the Church of the Transfiguration. The two youth groups they helped to lead continued to grow and become a real joy for all those involved. Ray and Cameron continually shared their humor with each other and the teenagers under their leadership. Together, they not only continued to drink a great deal of coffee, but they kept the humor going in both youth groups as well.

Ian and Brienne set a wedding date and were married in June at the Church of the Transfiguration with Alex officiating. Kelly was Brienne's matron of honor as she and Donald beat Ian and Brienne to the altar!

As for Rasmus Gilbert Feynman, his trip through the transfer portal was a swift and joyous one. On his return to the intermediate heaven, he was quick to report to Quintas. Entering Quintas' office, Rasmus stood at attention and gave Quintas a brisk earthly military salute. Quintas, this time, did not seem to mind as he was delighted with the outcome above the Allegheny River on planet Earth. "Well, my good saint, you get high marks for this one," stated Quintas, with a smile on his angelic face. "You completed every part of your assignment, and you left the Church of the Transfiguration in great shape! Well done! I repeat, well done! It is very interesting to me, and I think highly symbolic as well, that the church which honors the transfiguration of the Christ, along with the appearance of Elijah and Moses, experienced both a demonic twist to the story and your presence from Heaven as both a spiritual and physical manifestation. I guess that the Church of the Transfiguration had its own transfiguration. I certainly need to reflect more on that one! By the way, while you were on Earth, a new development occurred here in the heavenly realm. We received a new arrival with whom you are well acquainted. I have someone nearby who is just dying to see you! And you can take my language quite literally." With that statement, Quintas brought Kinghorn's canine spirit out to reunite with Rasmus.

"My Big Dog," exclaimed Rasmus holding out his arms with great glee. The two of them were overjoyed to see each other. Both of them danced and capered about! "My Big Dog has come back to me," Rasmus announced with glee. Addressing Quintas, Rasmus said, "When I was a little boy I had a stuffed animal – a dog that I named 'Big Dog'. I lost him while attending a parade with my great aunt and uncle. We went back to the spot where we watched the parade, but he was gone. I was heartbroken and suffered greatly from separation anxiety. I have always viewed Kinghorn as my Big Dog coming back to be with me. Lost again in death, we are now reunited in a new life."

Quintas spoke again, adding more details to the dog's heavenly advent as he continued to view the joy that had enveloped Rasmus and Kinghorn. "Your dog died on Christmas Day, much to the heartache of Laurel, John, and Janet. They are cremating him and received permission to bury him on top of your grave in Saxonburg. They thought you might appreciate that."

"Yes, I do," stated Rasmus. "That is a sweet and very thoughtful gesture. I am happy that they could arrange that!"

"Well, my saint – two more quality assignments like the one you just pulled off, and you will reach the level of an 'Ace' – an ace saint of the heavenly hosts for sure!"

"That is something I wouldn't mind securing, if you please," replied Rasmus. "Thank you, Quintas!"

With that, a happy Rasmus, and an even happier dog, left the office and were off to Rasmus' primary abode.

As we come to the conclusion of this story, Alex had one more task to perform that we absolutely must share with you, the reader, concerning this remarkable tale. If you remember, as Rasmus neared the end of his time with Father McKenzie, Rasmus requested a pen and paper. He wrote something down and asked Alex to make the delivery. Several days after Christmas, Alex travelled to Delmont to the home of Laurel Ann White Feynman. He had previously arranged the meeting, informing Laurel that he had a message for her, but did not share anything else about its contents or the author. Upon arrival, Laurel invited Alex to come in and have a seat in the living room. After exchanging some pleasantries, Alex proceeded to pass to Laurel the note he brought down with him from Plum Township. Laurel's eyes enlarged as she read the communication. She then began to cry. "How, how is this?" she asked.

"I don't quite know how to explain this to you, but over Christmas I made the acquaintance of your late husband," stated Alex sheepishly. "He was sent by Heaven to our parish to help us eradicate a demonic spirit who was creating havoc in the church and among our people, particularly one individual. He was successful in his mission and has returned to the intermediate heaven. The heavenly authorities, apparently, would not permit him to contact you and the children. I really do not know why. I think he wanted to communicate with you regardless of his heavenly directives and orders. Writing this note is the way I guess he chose to do it. It appears from the text that he wanted you to know that life and love goes on, and that he is waiting happily for your coming reunion. I am being totally honest with you about this. I am not making this up or playing a cruel joke on you. Believe me, I want nothing from you and I ask nothing of you!"

"No, I am not thinking that at all," responded Laurel.

At this, Alex explained the whole circumstance of the situation and how he had come to meet and work with the late Father Feynman. Laurel quietly wept throughout the whole conversation saying to Alex, "You have no idea how I do miss him so. This note is a great relief to me and fills me with a tremendous amount of joy and hope. I can guarantee you that this is truly Rasmus' signature. I will hold this piece of paper close to my heart and cherish it for the rest of my life."

The note from Rasmus to Laurel read:

"My Dearest Love,
In my life I have witnessed great love,
Special is your love which you have shared with me.
I have counselled love.
I have received counselling concerning love.

I have spoken love.
I have heard love spoken.
I have loved.
I have been loved
I will love again.
I will be loved again.
Love is eternal,
Love never falls, fails, or ends.
With love there can be no ultimate separation.
We will clothe one another with our mutual expression of love again.
I await your coming to me as the fire of my love burns bright for you.
I will be here waiting to love you in person forever and ever!
Live and love expectantly,
Your dear Rasmus."

Alex travelled back to Plum Township in total silence and contemplation. Returning to his office, his thoughts turned humorous. Leaning back in his swivel chair, his mind centered on the Warner Brothers' character of Porky Pig. Rising from his chair and preparing to go home, he said to no one in particular, "Th-th-th-that's all folks!"

RASMUS GILBERT FEYNMAN WILL RETURN!

About the Author

obert Cameron Malcolm IV is a 1973 graduate of Highlands High School, a 1977 graduate of Westminster College, New Wilmington, PA., and a 1981 graduate of Pittsburgh Theological Seminary. He served the First Presbyterian Church of Bentleyville, PA., for 6 ½ years. He served the Natrona Heights Presbyterian Church as pastor and youth group leader for 30 years from 1987 through 2017. This book is his fifth. Previously, he has produced a history of Natrona Heights Presbyterian Church and *Youth Groups My Way: Philosophy, Application, and Anthology.* He has also published, *Mary Magdalene: New Testament Eve, A Divine Christmas Ghost Story,* and *A Divine Christmas Ghost Story: Book Two.* Currently, he is working on three additional books. Cam lives in Natrona Heights with his wife, Laurie, and his son, Cameron. Please visit his Facebook page for details about his books and upcoming book events. You can also reach him by email at rc4malcolm@comcast.net.

WA